DEATH OF A SCAVENGER

DEATH OF A SCAVENGER

A JUNIPER GROVE MYSTERY

KARIN KAUFMAN

CHAPTER 1

Someone had centered the body on a thick wool blanket and arranged it in an unrealistic pose. Legs straight, arms folded across the stomach. Worse, the body fidgeted and spoke from time to time.

"Julia, dead bodies aren't supposed to move," I said with a chuckle.

"My nose itches," she replied. "Either I scratch it or you do, Rachel."

"Scratch away, but every time you move, that rubber knife in your chest wiggles."

"Why did I agree to do this?" Julia said as she relieved her itching nose.

Holly Kavanagh bent forward, leaning close to Julia's face, and nodded approvingly. "You make a lovely murder victim. And you're short enough to fit in among the pumpkins."

"Just find the clues so I can get up, will you?" Julia said.

"There are three more teams behind us," I reminded her. "You have to stay here until the last one has passed."

Julia rolled her eyes.

I shook the sheet of paper the scavenger hunt organizers had given each team. "Here we go. Ready, Team

Finch Hill?"

"First riddle?" Holly said, rubbing her palms together.

"It says, 'Where once was green, 'tis both red and bare. Look below, the weapon is there.'"

"That's an easy one," Holly said, looking at the maple tree in Eric and Olivia Seitz's front yard.

Grinning, we marched for the tree, swept aside a pile of fallen leaves, and found the murder weapon—a plastic table knife, its blade painted red. "Got it," Holly said triumphantly, dropping it into her backpack.

Laughter sounded farther up the street, where several teams had gone before us, and as I brushed leaves over the remaining plastic knives, four people raced by on the sidewalk.

"Are they jumping the queue?" Holly asked. "Teams are supposed to go in order."

"Maybe they're not in the hunt."

"Team Lookout will be here in five minutes," she warned.

"Having fun?" Eric Seitz called out from his porch. He put his drink down on a plant stand and waved. "I've got hot cider here for the contestants."

"Thanks for letting the scavenger committee use your yard for a brutal murder," I said, moving for the porch. "It's perfect. Autumn leaves, my next-door neighbor dead in the pumpkin patch."

Holly hissed at me. "Don't let him distract you with cider. His wife is on Team Main Street."

"Rachel Stowe, you get right back here," Julia said.

"Sorry, Eric," I said, jabbing a thumb over my shoulder. "The body orders me to keep looking for clues."

"Well, if the body orders," he said, reaching for his

6

cup. "Come back when the hunt's over if you want."

"We've got four minutes," Holly said. "We can't let the next team see us finding things. If they do, they won't have to solve the riddles themselves."

"This is supposed to be fun, not frantic," I said, giving the clue sheet another shake. "Here we go. 'Some call it Great, some slice it too. Look under its cap to find the next clue.'" I glanced at Holly. "A pumpkin. Find a carved pumpkin with its top on."

We began to dig among the pumpkins in the Seitzes' small patch, and I quickly found a carved one half-hidden under yellowed pumpkin leaves. I pulled off the top, reached inside, and retrieved a small slip of paper. "It says, 'Congratulations, now add this to your sack. To find the third clue, don't look back."

"Ohh," Holly said with a mock shiver. "Sounds like something out of a horror movie. *Don't look behind you.*"

"For goodness' sake," Julia said in a loud whisper. "The last clue is right in front of you."

"How do you know?" I said.

"The committee was still placing clues when I got here."

"That's cheating, isn't it?" Holly said, a mischievous twinkle in her eye. "I think we have to forfeit several minutes."

Julia raised herself on her elbows. "Rachel Stowe and Holly Kavanagh, I'm in my sixties, and I'm not going to lie in the dark on this cold ground one minute more than I have to. If you want to stay friends, you'll stop fooling around and look behind that pumpkin right now."

I did as instructed, crouching down and parting the dry pumpkin leaves. "Rubber spiders," I said, grabbing one and handing it to Holly. "It's got a tag around its abdomen. Are you really cold, Julia?"

"No, I'm fine," Julia answered. "I just feel ridiculous. I didn't think I would, but I do."

"The tag reads, 'Put the spider in your bag, then leave this place to see the hag,'" Holly said.

"The hag?" I said.

"Who or what is the hag?" Holly said.

"I'm afraid I can't help with the next checkpoint," Julia said.

I stood straight. "I'll bet it's a Halloween decoration."

Holly put the slip of paper and the spider in her backpack. "There's a house two blocks up that always does it up royally this time of year. Scarecrows, lots of jack-o'-lanterns. Maybe they have a witch this year."

We dashed up the street, Julia shouting after us to hurry up and win so she could go home. One block into our dash, a woman on her porch waved us down, insisting we stop. "Hello! Rachel, isn't it?"

"Gina." I came to a halt. "Gina Peeler, right?"

"We're in the scavenger hunt," Holly said. She addressed Gina but continued to move ahead, tugging imploringly at my sleeve.

"That's why I stopped you," Gina said. She waved at us again, this time motioning for us to enter her yard through her picket-fence gate.

Holly, eager to beat Team Main Street, groaned as I opened the gate and strode to Gina's porch. I'd met Gina twice before, three months ago, and though I'd momentarily forgotten her last name, I had no trouble remembering her or her house.

I sidestepped dead and dying pumpkin leaves and

stems on my way up her brick path, marveling at how many people in Juniper Grove had pumpkin patches in their front yards. Twelve hundred people in our small town, and I'd already seen three such yards on just this one street.

"You've got a great view of the hunt," I said, climbing her steps.

"I can't participate," Gina answered, giving her cane a thump on the concrete porch, "but this is the next best thing. It's more entertaining than television." Her gray hair was half low ponytail, half dreadlocks, and she played with the turquoise beads on the latter as she commanded me to sit on the plastic patio chair next to hers. "I believe I'm the hag," she said, smiling sheepishly.

Holly darted up the steps and took the seat next to mine. "You are?"

"I'm not supposed to know, but three teams have passed by asking me if I know who or what the 'hag' is, and a couple hours ago, when I was inside fixing a mug of tea, I saw two people hiding something behind my largest pumpkin, next to the red barberry."

I looked out over her front yard. "What were they hiding?"

"Witch hats with tags on them. I didn't read the tags." She shrugged. "I went back to my tea."

It took me a second to recover from her reply. If it had been me, I would have flown out of my house and asked who those people were and what on earth they thought they were doing. "The committee isn't supposed to use a yard without the permission of the owner."

"I think I'm an exception, like I usually am around Halloween." She grimaced slightly as she shifted in her chair, taking pressure off one hip and putting it on the other.

"This is my first autumn in Juniper Grove."

"I remember now. You're the newcomer to Colorado."

"No, I'm a native, but I lived in Boston for seven years."

"In exile out East, eh?"

"I guess you could say that. I've been in Juniper Grove for five months now."

"Well, I'm the creepy woman with the cane. Kids enjoy spooky stories this time of year, and I don't mind helping them out."

It was beginning to dawn on me. Gina was the subject of an unkind scavenger joke. "So the committee used your house without your permission? And teams are supposed to figure out—"

"Who the hag is," she finished. "But here's the thing. None of the teams have figured it out yet, and I haven't said a word to anyone but you two about the witch hats."

A breeze caught a pair of wind chimes hanging from her soffit, and their bamboo tubes played a soft melody that rose above the chatter of game players on the sidewalk. I didn't believe Gina's smile for one second. She was a sweet woman who wore mismatched socks, lived in a bright yellow house, and never seemed to leave her porch, but she was kind and interesting and fun. And now she was a cruel riddle in a town scavenger hunt. Suddenly I didn't feel like playing.

"Rachel, according to the rules, homeowners can help stumped players by giving them additional clues," Gina said. "Since no one asked my permission or gave me additional clues, I'm making them up myself. You and your friend can beat all the other teams."

Gina was beaming. In a small way, it seemed, helping Team Finch Hill was her revenge for the riddle.

Holly leaned forward in her chair. "I'm Holly Kavanagh, by the way. I own the bakery downtown."

"Fabulous pastries," Gina said. "I have a neighbor who brings me a box of almond scones every other Monday. She gave me one just this morning."

I turned to Holly. "Let's do it."

I didn't have to say it twice. I thanked Gina, told her I'd see her later in the week, then ran after Holly as she hurried for the barberry shrub, which still wore half its deep red leaves. We stopped and glanced about. Seeing that no one else was near, we bent down and rummaged behind the large pumpkin next to the shrub. "Found a hat," I said.

"We should leave Gina's yard before we read the clue," Holly said, yanking the strap of her backpack back onto her shoulder.

"And then let's find out who on the committee made up that nasty riddle."

"Agreed."

On the sidewalk three houses down, I opened the tag attached to our witch hat. "It says, 'Who killed the woman, knife in her chest? To ask the witness, go to the nest.'"

Holly and I stared at each other.

"What nest?" Holly said. "I don't mind hard clues, but I do mind if they're unsolvable."

Three boys in their late teens bounded by, excitement written on their faces. "I told ya it would be better this year!" one said as he pocketed his cell phone.

Holly put a hand on her hip. "Are they cheating?"

"We kind of cheated."

"Not technically. Gina was allowed to help us."

Four women sprinted toward us on the sidewalk, moving as though they had just discovered the answer to the

11

tenth annual Juniper Grove Murder Mystery Scavenger Hunt. Before we had a chance to get out of their way, they split into two pairs, swung around us, rejoined, and then raced off in the same direction as the teenagers.

"We're the only ones who have this nest clue," I said, "so where's everyone going?"

"There's one way to find out," Holly said, once more taking off ahead of me.

Two blocks down on the same side of the street, a crowd had gathered in the front yard of a two-story house, their eyes trained on something in the yard's small pumpkin patch. As I weaved my way forward, a woman turned back, shaking her head. "That's Maureen Nicholson," she said.

"She has a piece of paper in her hand," another woman said. "It's a riddle about a robin's egg. Our team didn't have that riddle, did yours?"

"Someone texted me that they added a second body to the hunt," I heard a man say.

"It took me a minute to realize," an elderly man said. "I just thought it was very realistic. The poor woman."

I found Holly at the front of the crowd, gazing with horror at a lifeless body angled between the pumpkins.

"Did someone check her pulse?" a woman asked.

But it was clear from Maureen Nicholson's open and glazed eyes that she was dead. And of course there was the knife. A large one with a black handle protruded from her chest. And it wasn't rubber.

CHAPTER 2

Police Chief James Gilroy scowled and mumbled as Officer Derek Underhill cordoned off the crime scene with yellow tape. We had all made a mess of the scene, Julia included. On hearing whispers of a murder four blocks away, she'd left her duties as the hunt's body to join the crowd. Twenty or more of us, stomping, poking, touching. One man even admitted to touching the knife in Maureen's chest, thinking it was a joke. He said he realized it was real the moment he touched it.

Gilroy ordered us not to leave and herded us into the next yard, where we hugged the low picket fence, watching Underhill do his work. I figured he couldn't legally tell us to move even farther away, especially since the owners of the lawn on which we were standing were also observing the goings-on behind the fence.

The chief strode up the concrete walk to the house next door and knocked hard on its double green doors. No one answered, which didn't surprise me. If anyone had been home, they would have heard the commotion long ago and stepped outside.

As Gilroy headed back to Underhill, a woman called out, "The Andersons live there, but they're out celebrating their anniversary."

"Thank you," Gilroy said with barely a backward

glance.

Gilroy didn't like an audience at a murder scene—what police chief would?—but from our vantage point, Maureen's body was obscured by huge pumpkins and dead or dying pumpkin vines.

"What's with all the pumpkin patches in Juniper Grove?" I asked Holly.

"We have two contests every October, one for the biggest pumpkin and one for the best carved jack-o'-lantern. It's sort of a big deal."

"I've never heard anything about these contests."

"The downtown merchants' organization runs them."

A forty-something woman, her short dark hair like a smooth cap atop her head, sidled up to Holly, nudged her, and said, "I guess your competition is over." She instantly clamped a hand over her mouth.

Holly stared at her, incredulous. "Olivia, that's a terrible thing to say!"

The woman dropped her manicured hand, acknowledging her embarrassment with a nod. "I'm so sorry. It just came out. I don't know why I did that. I just . . . I know Maureen had it out for you and your bakery, and I . . ."

"I know," Holly said. "Never mind. Olivia, this is my friend Rachel Stowe, and you know Julia. Rachel, this is Olivia Seitz. She owns Blooms on Main Street."

"I thought I recognized you," I said. "I've been to Blooms several times."

"That's good to know," Olivia said. "We sell stationery now too."

"I'll have to take a look."

"I just bought some lovely blue stationery there," Holly said.

"And their Christmas card selection is excellent," Julia said.

It was an odd conversation, considering where we were, so the four of us fell silent and looked away, off to where Maureen Nicholson's body lay among the pumpkins.

As harsh as Olivia Seitz's comments on Holly's competition had been, they were true. Everyone knew that Maureen's brand-new drive-through shop, Coffee and Cakes, was a direct threat to Holly's bakery. Coffee and Cakes was the fast-food equivalent of Holly's Sweets. Customers didn't even have to leave their cars for a hot coffee and scone. Just drive up and load up. Still, Holly had never panicked. She knew she was a top-notch baker. Maureen may have had speed, but Holly had quality.

My attention shifted to Chief Gilroy, who had crouched near the body, his back to the crowd. I hadn't seen him in three weeks, even though I'd taken numerous strolls downtown, deliberately slowing and even hovering by the police station. He'd been on my mind for more than a month, since I'd solved, or kind of solved, the case of missing-then-dead George Foster, my friend Julia's estranged husband. Maybe he'd had time to rethink his admiration of my investigative prowess.

Not that it mattered. I was attracted to him, though I'd never conceded as much to Holly and Julia, but as I told myself again and again, I wasn't in his ballpark. He was forty-eight and I was forty-three, and we both had dark hair with creeping touches of gray, but there the ballpark-ness ended. He was trim, with the iciest blue eyes I'd ever seen, and had a commanding and confident air about him—which at times verged on aloofness. I was twenty pounds or more overweight, joyfully sloppy when it came to clothes, and lacked in the confidence department. Neither of us was going to change.

"Maureen's husband is out of town," Olivia said, exaggerating a grimace. "I don't think anyone knows where."

Julia shook her head. "I saw him downtown this afternoon."

"Kirk Nicholson? Mid-forties, brown hair, big nose?" Olivia asked, clearly questioning either Julia's eyesight or memory.

"I know what he looks like, Olivia," Julia replied. "He was coming out of an office building downtown."

Olivia's brow wrinkled. "That's funny." Seemingly confounded by the information, she tucked a strand of short brown hair behind her ear and stared off into the distance, lost until Julia brought her back to the conversation.

"There's no confusing Kirk Nicholson with anyone else. I'm positive it was him. About two o'clock, outside the office building next to Town Hall."

"Maureen told me this morning he was out of town and wouldn't be back for a week," Olivia said.

"Either she lied or she doesn't keep tabs on her husband," Julia said, never one to mince words.

The coroner's van pulled to the curb. In a few minutes he'd remove Maureen's body, and Gilroy and Underhill would start questioning us. I motioned for Holly, Julia, and Olivia to follow me as I backed away from the fence and the crowd's prying ears.

"What about this riddle?" I asked, taking a wrinkled bit of paper from my jacket pocket. "Did anyone else see this? 'Blue like a robin's egg, under the tree. Look for it now, it holds the key.'"

"Where did you get that?" Julia asked.

"When I first got here, I saw Maureen holding a sheet of paper, printed out on a computer. A woman in the crowd managed to read the paper, and I wrote down what it said while she could still remember. Did you get this on your team, Olivia?"

Olivia unfolded her clue list and showed it to me. It looked exactly like Team Finch Hill's, with three clues at each checkpoint and seven checkpoints in all. "I don't know where Maureen would have gotten another clue—or why. She was on Team Main Street with me and Tyler and Jenny Hannaford."

"Why didn't Eric join the hunt?" Holly asked.

"He's at home on our porch, trying to slow the other teams with promises of hot cider."

Holly turned to me. "I told you."

"Did Maureen go off on her own?" I asked Olivia.

"She must have."

"Do you remember when?"

"I wasn't paying attention. We were at the third checkpoint when I realized she was gone. To be real, I didn't care when or why she left, I was just glad she had. I knew we'd have a happier night without her."

Seemingly uncomfortable with Olivia's bluntness, Holly made a face.

"Come on, Holly, you know what she was like," Olivia said. "I thought she left us to form Team Maureen Nicholson and win the hunt all by herself."

"Had she done that before?" I asked.

"She never joined in the scavenger hunt until tonight," Olivia answered. "I was shocked when she asked to join Team Main Street, though I guess it made sense with her opening Coffee and Cakes. She wanted to be part of the business community."

"She *was* part," Holly said.

Olivia frowned. "I don't know why you defend her. She was ruthless in everything she did, and her number one goal was to close your bakery. You know what she told me? She said with Holly's Sweets gone, her business would explode and she could create a franchise. You knew her, Julia. Tell me I'm wrong."

"I think . . ." Julia made a faint backward gesture with her hand in the direction of Maureen's body. "She's over there, dead now."

"Someone murdered her," Olivia said. "It was bound to happen."

"Ladies?"

I'd been so engrossed in Olivia's words and what they might mean that I hadn't noticed Chief Gilroy approach. Notebook and pen in hand, he proceeded to question us, calling me "Miss Stowe" again, though I'd asked him a month ago to tone it down to a simple "Rachel." Now in October, we were back to the formality of September.

"Do any of you know who would want to harm Mrs. Nicholson?" he asked.

Olivia guffawed. "I'd say half the town."

"I understand she was on your team during the scavenger hunt, Mrs. Seitz," Gilroy said.

"*We* didn't kill her," Olivia said.

"But half the town wanted to?"

"I was making a point."

"She wasn't well liked," Gilroy stated flatly.

"She wasn't, Chief Gilroy," Julia said. "I'm afraid what Olivia says is true. Maureen Nicholson was an unpleasant woman, and I'm sure she was an unhappy one."

"Why unhappy?"

"Aren't most unpleasant people unhappy?" Julia said.

"Even Caleb had a run-in with her, didn't he?" Olivia said, turning to Holly.

Dumbstruck, Holly latched on to her long, dark ponytail and pulled it over her shoulder, a habit that somehow made her look younger than her thirty-seven years. "Caleb is thirteen."

"I mean, he's a good boy," Olivia continued. "Not like some of the kids around here. You could believe there'd be bad blood between them and Olivia, but not Caleb. He's not one of those nasty kids. That's what I'm saying."

I'd briefly met Olivia Seitz before, a couple of times, but I didn't really know her, so maybe it was just her way, I thought. She didn't *mean* to make sneaky, backhanded allegations.

Holly fixed her eyes on Gilroy, her small, delicate features hardening to stone. "Maureen accused Caleb of throwing eggs at her front door last week. He didn't. He didn't even go out that night."

"Fine," Gilroy said. He glanced down at our feet. "You all have bags of some kind, is that right?"

"For collecting clues," Olivia said. "One member on each team carries one."

"And where is yours, Mrs. Seitz?"

"Umm . . ." Olivia scanned the crowd. "There they are. Tyler, Jenny," she called out as she waved at a couple.

As if begging recognition for the inconvenience she was suffering, the woman pouted and shuffled up to Gilroy. "We were already questioned," she said before he could speak.

19

"I need to see inside that bag, please," Gilroy said.

"It's my daughter's backpack," the woman corrected, tossing back her blonde hair. "We already showed the other officer."

The man beside her let loose a long sigh. "Jenny, just open it so we can go home. I'm tired."

Jenny was in her late thirties, I guessed, and the man—I knew him to be her husband—was maybe a year or two older. I'd seen them before, but I couldn't recall where, though I thought it had something to do with Holly and her bakery.

"Your names?" Gilroy said.

"I'm Tyler Hannaford, and this is my wife, Jenny. We were part of Team Main Street with Olivia."

Jenny Hannaford unzipped her backpack and watched with distaste as Gilroy slipped on a pair of gloves and inspected every inch of the bag with his flashlight.

Job done, Gilroy slipped his flashlight into his coat. "Please turn out the pockets in your coats and pants," he said. "You too, ladies."

"This is getting offensive," Jenny said.

"I understand," Gilroy said.

We all did as the chief asked, but truth be told, I was feeling a little offended myself. Sure, it was Gilroy's job, and he'd have been a fool to let us go without checking our pockets for something incriminating, but I felt faintly ill standing there with my pockets turned out, especially after the wrinkled bit of paper I'd written the robin's egg clue on fell out.

"That's a scavenger riddle," I said in answer to Gilroy's questioning look.

He picked it up. "This is familiar."

20

"I made note of the riddle in Maureen Nicholson's hand."

He didn't scowl or reprimand. He simply continued as though he hadn't seen the paper at all. But when he handed it back to me, I felt his disapproval.

"What team were you on, Miss Stowe?" he asked.

"Team Finch Hill, for the name of our street. Just me and Holly."

"I need to see your bag."

"I've got it," Holly said, twisting back. "Or at least I thought I did."

I pointed. "Next to the fence."

Holly jogged to the fence, returned with the backpack, and unzipped the main opening and one of the two side pockets. The second pocket, I saw, was already open. Gilroy knelt and began his flashlight inspection.

"Can we go now, Chief?" Tyler Hannaford asked.

"I'll need to talk to you both tomorrow," Gilroy said, looking up at the couple.

"We both work downtown," Jenny said. "Can we stop by the station?"

"That's fine," Gilroy said as he returned to his inspection. "Thank you for staying."

Jenny rolled her eyes in dramatic fashion, letting everyone but Gilroy know how put out she was by the whole unseemly ordeal, then took her husband's arm and headed off into the night.

"Mrs. Kavanagh?" Gilroy said, peering into one of the backpack's side pockets.

"I think I left the zipper on that pocket open," Holly said. She looked to me. "Didn't I?"

Gilroy slid his hand inside the pocket, retrieved what

21

looked like a small computer flash drive, and illuminated it with his flashlight. It was a bright blue metal drive—smudged with red.

"Is that blood?" Olivia said. "It *is*. It's blood."

CHAPTER 3

"Do you think Holly went to the bakery this morning?" Julia asked.

"Knowing Holly, she probably did," I said. I took a last bite of toast, carried my plate to the sink, and started the coffeemaker. "Coffee?"

"Yes, two or three cups." Julia absentmindedly played with a curl of her short gray hair.

Both of us were worried about Holly, and we could hardly wrap our minds around what had happened last night. Not just Maureen Nicholson's murder, but also the discovery of that computer drive. How had a bloody flash drive ended up in Holly's backpack? After confiscating the backpack and extracting a promise from Holly that she'd pay a visit to the police station this morning, Gilroy had let her go home, much to the consternation of Olivia Seitz.

"That wasn't Holly's drive," Julia said.

"Of course it wasn't."

"She left one of the pockets of her backpack unzipped and someone put it there."

"Or someone unzipped the pocket, dropped the drive, and forgot to zip it back up."

"Olivia wanted Holly arrested on the spot."

"We don't even know whose blood was on the drive."

Julia stopped twirling her hair. "We can make an

23

educated guess."

I had to agree. I'd been grasping at straws in my mind, coming up with all kinds of unlikely scenarios for the blood and for the presence of the drive itself. It was Caleb's flash drive, and he'd accidentally cut himself, touched the drive, and put it in the wrong backpack. Or someone cut his finger during the scavenger hunt, pulled the drive out of his pocket for some reason, and mistakenly dropped it into the wrong backpack. Neither scenario held up to any scrutiny.

I handed Julia her first cup of coffee and joined her at my kitchen table. "Did you see Holly's face? She went white."

"Chief Gilroy's not going to arrest her, is he?"

I hesitated before answering, setting Julia off on a rant.

"Tell me he would *never* do that. He's not a stupid man, and Holly's no murderer. Gilroy knows that. Everyone knows that. I'm telling you, if he arrests her, if he so much as talks about arresting her, I'll be at the station with a pitchfork."

"I don't think it will come to that," I said, trying to sound more confident than I was. If the blood on the drive turned out to be Maureen's, would Gilroy have a choice? Then again, he hadn't arrested Julia in September, even when ordered to by the town attorney. He wasn't a capricious man. "I could tell Gilroy thought there was something fishy going on with that drive, and that it didn't involve Holly. He's not going to arrest her just because it was in her backpack. He'd need more evidence than that."

"He's not going to find more evidence," Julia said. "Not with Holly, he isn't."

I wrapped my fingers around my coffee cup and felt a slight shiver. My house was too cold. Just last week the weather had taken a sudden turn from Indian summer to full-fledged autumn, and in five days it would be November. "Do you think the kids will still go trick-or-treating?"

"Would you send a child out on Halloween night with a knife-wielding murderer on the loose?"

"When you put it that way, no."

"At this very moment, Olivia Seitz is spreading lies about Holly and that drive."

I nodded. "I know she is." I'd met Olivia twice before, I thought. Both times in her store. And both times she had smiled, commented on the weather, and moved on. A pleasant woman. But last night, during my first real conversation with her, I'd seen a side of her character I thoroughly disliked. "Bringing up Caleb's trouble with Maureen was pretty sneaky."

"Holly handled it well." Julia took a long, lingering sip of coffee and then set down her cup. "What are we going to do?"

"I'm thinking about that."

"Are you?" Julia breathed a sigh of relief. "I was hoping you were. Holly is devastated, and I know Caleb is going to be bullied at school over this. Olivia will make sure of that." She rapped the tabletop. "We have to help them. We're the ones who were there. We heard and saw things the police didn't."

"So did Eric Seitz and Gina Peeler, from their porches."

"I wouldn't trust Eric to be observant, but Gina is a smart woman, and she sees things going on in the neighborhood that no one else does."

"How long have you known her?"

"Ten, eleven years. I don't know her well, I just know

she's sharp."

"How old is she?"

"Mid-fifties, I think."

"You're joking." Julia's answer shocked me. I had judged her to be in her late sixties. "She looks so much older."

"She's had a tough life."

"Why does she use a cane?"

"She was in a car accident before she moved here, but I've never asked her for details."

I told Julia about the hag clue, and that Gina knew the clue was about her and had gone out of her way to help Holly and me with the hunt. "There's something else I want to investigate while I'm at it. Who thought it would be okay to plant that clue in Gina's yard?"

Julia quickly downed the rest of her coffee and requested a second cup. While I poured and then retook my seat, she told me she'd overheard a strange conversation between Jenny Hannaford and Olivia Seitz while playing the scavenger hunt's body.

"I think they honestly forgot I was alive and could hear them. They were talking about the pumpkin-carving contest last week. Maureen got the blue ribbon, but according to Jenny, she cheated."

"How do you cheat at pumpkin carving?"

"Jenny claimed that Maureen brought in someone else to do the carving, and I have to say, after looking at the photo of her winning pumpkin in the paper, unless Maureen has extraordinary talents and a lot of time on her hands, I agree with Jenny."

"That's silly."

"Have you seen the photo?"

"No, I mean the whole thing is silly, Julia. Why would anyone care?"

"Some people take the contest very seriously. They grow their own pumpkins, feed them special fertilizers all summer long, shade them from the hot afternoon sun with white sheets. Justin Miller won the last two years in a row, before Maureen took over. Though he won for biggest pumpkin this year, so he wasn't completely left out. Maureen doesn't grow her own."

I sipped at my coffee, hiding a smile behind my cup. I liked pumpkins and contests, but this was taking both to extremes.

"You can laugh, but how do you know Maureen wasn't killed because of the contest?"

I *thought* I'd hidden my smile. "Justin Miller would kill Maureen over a pumpkin cheat?"

"Justin disliked Maureen as much as most people in Juniper Grove. If she took the title away from him, it could have pushed him over the edge."

"The title?" This was too much. I had to laugh. "I've met Justin Miller, and he doesn't strike me as unhinged." Justin owned the Porter Grill, a steakhouse on the eastern edge of downtown. I'd never eaten there, but Holly spoke well of it.

"He's a very nice man, but Maureen pushed people too far."

I reconsidered. What was silly to some could be important to others, and people had murdered over lesser things than lost contests. "Was Justin in the scavenger hunt?"

"I didn't see him, and everyone who played had to start at my checkpoint, so I got a good look."

"That doesn't mean he wasn't there. We don't know

27

how many people were actually playing and how many were just out for the night. I need to make a list."

"I thought you'd never say. Where are your notepads?"

I laughed. Julia knew my methods. Write everything down on a yellow legal pad. Make lists. Then put everything—photos, maps, the smallest scrap of detail—on a giant corkboard I used to plot my mystery novels, where I could see the whole picture at a glance. After seven long years as a book editor in Boston, I'd left the big city for little Juniper Grove. I'd wanted to live in Colorado again—and to try my hand at writing mysteries for a living. I'd sold my first book before leaving Boston, which perhaps set my expectations foolishly high, but with my savings and a small inheritance from my parents—not to mention no husband or children to spend money on—I'd be okay for a while.

"Let's go to Gina's house first," I said, setting my cup in the sink. "I need more information."

"Do you think Chief Gilroy will object to you investigating?"

"James Gilroy can't tell me not to talk to people. That's outside his job description."

"I think he likes you, Rachel."

"Oh, Julia," I moaned, "you think every unattached man in Juniper Grove likes me."

"My nephew does."

"The fact is, until last night I hadn't seen Gilroy in three weeks. What does that tell you?"

"It tells me he's a busy man, and for that you should be glad. Do you know how many bums there are these days? Chief Gilroy is decent, and smart, and in case you hadn't noticed, good looking."

I heard another Gilroy Rhapsody coming on, and

hoping to put a quick end to it, I grabbed my jacket and car keys and took off for the back door. "Coming?" I called. "Don't forget your jacket."

By the time I'd backed out of my backyard detached garage and turned onto Finch Hill Road, Julia had forgiven my rude exit. I suggested we make a stop downtown, at Holly's Sweets, before driving to Gina's house. It was after nine in the morning now, just past the bakery's busiest hours, and I wanted to talk to Holly before she paid Chief Gilroy a visit.

It was obvious from the moment we walked through the front door that Holly's morning wasn't going at all well. Head down, she scrubbed away at a countertop and only reluctantly stopped her work to look up. The relief in her expression was obvious.

"Who did you think we were?" I asked, stepping to the counter.

She tossed her sponge like a Frisbee and watched it land on the microwave behind her. "Let's just say I'm not fond of some people and their children this morning."

"What happened?" Julia asked.

"Some of the kids at Caleb's school called me a murderer."

"Oh, poor Caleb," I said. "That must have upset him."

"He wanted to come home, but Peter talked him into staying. He told him it would only get worse if he left, but I'm not sure we made the right decision."

"The kids will get bored soon and move on to something new," Julia said.

"It's not just the kids," Holly said, leaning on the counter. "Those kids weren't even at the scavenger hunt. They heard that I was a murderer from their parents."

Julia gave Holly's arm a quick pat. "Never mind. There will always be gossips. Besides, Rachel is on the case."

Holly stood straight. "I was going to ask you."

"I'm not promising anything, and anyway, Gilroy is on the case too."

"He's slow as molasses," Holly replied. "I can't wait for him to figure it out."

I glanced at the bakery's door. "I wanted to ask you something before anyone else came in. Did you set down your backpack anywhere else but by the fence last night?"

Holly tilted back her head as she thought about my question. "I set it down at the first checkpoint, where Julia's body was, but we were the only ones there. And I set it down on the sidewalk outside Gina Peeler's house, but only for a minute."

I remembered now. We had paused on the sidewalk, several houses down from Gina's. "Three teenage boys, or maybe they were in their early twenties, went around us, and a little later, four women went around us. But I don't see how any of them could have dropped the drive in your backpack. Was it open?"

"Probably, but none of them was close enough to drop it in, were they? They went around us."

"Maybe one of them tossed it and it just happened to land in your bag?" I immediately shook my head. No such miraculous toss had happened. "They were all heading in the direction of Maureen's body, and by then Maureen was already dead. I remember the boys were excited. I think one of them had just gotten a text message about Maureen."

"Everyone thought she was part of the hunt," Julia said.

"That drive was placed in your backpack when you set it down by the picket fence," I said. "Which means

Maureen's killer was there when we got there."

I recalled the expression on Gilroy's face when he found the drive and held it up to the light. He was surprised he'd found it in Holly's backpack and didn't believe for one moment that it was hers.

"The drive was blue," I said.

"I know," Holly said. "It's burned into my memory."

"No, I think that's it! Remember the riddle in Maureen's hand? 'Blue like a robin's egg, under the tree. Look for it now, it holds the key.' That's the blue flash drive. It has to be. Someone sent Maureen on her own scavenger hunt."

CHAPTER 4

When Julia and I arrived at Gina Peeler's house, she was on the porch of her bright yellow house, wrapped in a sweater and drinking from a shockingly orange mug. She was genuinely happy to see us, it seemed, and waved us in through the garden gate. As we headed for her porch, wading through the fallen leaves, I noticed that although her pumpkin vines had shriveled, her small pumpkin patch was untrampled—unlike her next-door neighbor's after last night's hunt. But then, only Holly and I had discovered the secret of the scavenger committee's unkind "hag" clue, and so we had been the only scavengers to visit Gina's yard. The paper witch hats were probably still behind that pumpkin.

"Good morning," Gina said, lifting her mug in a toast. "It's a beautiful fall day. Would you like some cinnamon tea? There's more in the Brown Betty pot, and you're welcome to go inside and get yourself some."

"No, thank you," Julia said. She sat primly in one of Gina's plastic chairs.

"I'd love some," I replied. As I opened the screen door, I looked back at Julia and caught sight of her skittish expression. "Sure you don't want some tea, Julia?"

"Thank you, but no."

I almost laughed. Julia was one of the kindest women I'd ever known, but she had a "proper" side to her that found

Gina and her house a little outside the bounds of decorum. On the other hand, though neither dreadlocks nor bright yellow paint were my style, I liked both Gina and her house, and I felt at ease in her presence, as though I'd known her for a long time.

The inside of Gina's house was no less bright than the outside. It was white and yellow and full of sunshine streaming in through her curtainless windows. The floor plan was backward, with the kitchen in the front of the house and what looked like the living room at the back. There were more wind chimes inside, too, by an open window over the kitchen sink.

I found her brown teapot, poured myself a mug of strong, dark, cinnamon tea, and went back out onto the porch.

Gina didn't waste any time on trivialities. "Are you investigating Maureen Nicholson's murder?" she asked as soon as I took the chair next to hers.

"You get right to the point," I said with a laugh.

"Life is too short to beat around the bush. You want to know what I saw."

I decided to dispense with the usual social preliminaries and get right to my questions. Not only would Gina not mind, but it appeared she'd prefer it. "Did you see or hear anything you think is important?"

"I've been thinking about it," Gina answered. "Going over the night in my mind. Who I remember walking past my house or asking me who the hag is."

"And who do you remember?" I asked.

"Well, that's the trouble. Probably a dozen people." Gina set down her cup on another plastic chair. "Though I know Maureen was one of them."

33

I sat forward. "She asked you who the hag is?"

"No, she asked me if I knew the meaning of a riddle. It was an odd clue no one else had—or at least no one else asked me about."

"About a blue robin's egg?"

Gina smiled and pointed her rather wrinkled forefinger at me. "You got it."

"That means someone handed her that clue early on in the hunt, probably at the first checkpoint," I said, turning to Julia.

"Everyone in the hunt started at my checkpoint, but I had my eyes closed most of the time," Julia said. "I heard things, but I didn't see much until you and Holly got there."

"Which made your checkpoint the perfect place to give her the clue," I said.

"Have you figured out what the riddle means?" Gina asked.

"I think it referred to a blue flash drive," I said. "Chief Gilroy found it in Holly's backpack."

"With blood on it," Julia added.

"Ah." Gina retrieved her mug and took a sip of tea, seemingly lost in thought.

"Did you see who the two people were who hid the witch hats in your yard?"

"It was Tyler and Jenny Hannaford, about an hour before the hunt started, though I can't be positive on the time."

"Were they on the scavenger hunt committee?" I asked.

"Committee members aren't allowed to participate in the hunt," Julia said.

"So why would they plant the hats?" I said.

"I can guess," Gina said. "My house wasn't on the official list, right? What a fabulous way to win the hunt. You send everyone else on a false clue."

"If that's true, then Tyler and Jenny told Olivia Seitz the hag clue was false. They were all on Team Main Street."

Gina nodded. "I don't remember Olivia asking me about the clue, so that could be. She wouldn't ask if she already knew the clue was meant to misdirect the other players."

The cinnamon taste was strong, almost biting, in Gina's tea. As I timidly sipped at it, I looked across the street to her neighbors' houses. No one else sat on a porch, though with the weather turning cold, that perhaps wasn't surprising, and besides, it was Tuesday, a work day for most people. "Gina, was anyone else, like in the houses across the street, watching the hunt?"

"People don't sit on their front porches as much as they used to, you know?" Gina's voice had a melancholy edge to it. "I didn't see a soul except for the scavengers."

"I sit on my porch," Julia said with pride. "And so does Rachel."

"I like to survey my little rose garden kingdom," I said.

"I know exactly what you mean," Gina said.

"Do you have any idea why anyone would want to kill Maureen?" I asked.

For a moment, Gina said nothing. She played with the beads in one of her dreadlocks, and then, as though she'd suddenly resolved to tell me a secret, she quietly said, "I can think of a lot of people."

"Like who?"

"Well, let's see. We can start with Justin Miller. You know he owns the Porter Grill?"

"Sure, I know."

"Good place, his pride and joy. So guess what Maureen Nicholson does? After she opens her Coffee and Cakes drive-through, of course." Gina set down her mug again. She was a hand talker, and she was in full swing. "She called the Health Department on him about ten days ago, claimed she saw mouse droppings in his restaurant."

"Never!" Julia said. "The Porter Grill is spotless!"

"I'll bet it is," Gina said. "I've never been there myself, but if I know Justin, and I do, you could eat off the floor. But Maureen called, and the Health Department inspectors had to go out there. Now, here's the thing. Once they're called, even if it's on a phony complaint, people can look that up. So the Porter Grill has a record now, like a criminal, and Justin has to let these inspectors in his door. And they do a big-time inspection of everything. They're shining flashlights into corners, looking behind refrigerators, under the sinks."

"Did they find anything?" I asked.

"Not a thing. He passed the inspection without a hitch."

"He must have been furious," Julia said.

"So would anyone. What if the inspectors had caught him at an off time and he hadn't passed? And how many people know now that someone complained of mouse droppings at his restaurant? Reputation is all in that business."

"Wait a minute," I said. "How would Justin know who called in the complaint? The Health Department wouldn't share Maureen's name with him."

"Justin has friends in the department," Gina said, putting her fingers over her lips in a gesture that called for our silence on the matter. "My neighbor, the one who brings

36

me Holly's scones, told me. She eats regularly at the Porter Grill and had a long talk with Justin. He knows what happened and who did it."

"But why would Maureen do that?" I said. "The Porter Grill doesn't even compete with Coffee and Cakes."

"Maureen was the sort of person who thought everything was a contest." Gina shrugged. "Maybe there was another reason, but from what my neighbor told me, Maureen was trying to damage anyone in competition with her."

It was hard to fathom that someone could be so blinded by ambition as to destroy someone's livelihood, but this wasn't the first time I'd heard how coldhearted Maureen was. "Last night Olivia said Maureen was ruthless, and that she was trying to ruin Holly's bakery."

Gina gave me a questioning look. "It sounds like Holly didn't tell you what Maureen did."

Julia shot forward in her chair. "What did she do?"

"Spread rumors that Holly's Sweets had failed a Health Department inspection. You didn't know?"

I was incredulous. "When?"

"It was about three weeks after Coffee and Cakes opened, so about a week ago. Holly didn't tell you?"

It was just like Holly not to say anything. She had probably dealt with it quickly and didn't want me or Julia to worry. "Justin Miller's friend in the department found out about this?"

"Someone told him, whether it was his friend or not, and my neighbor says Justin told Holly that it was Maureen."

Forgetting for an instant that Maureen was dead, I said, "What on earth is wrong with that woman?"

"Not to be mean," Gina said, "but whatever was wrong

with her is fixed now."

"This isn't good for Holly," Julia said. "Chief Gilroy is going to find out."

Gina shifted gingerly in her chair. "It has the appearance of a motive. And I'll tell you who else has a motive. Jenny Hannaford. There was trouble between her and Maureen in the Juniper Grove Vegetarian Society."

"You've got to be kidding me." Trouble among vegetarians sounded incongruous in a humorous kind of way, but I was willing to explore any avenue to help Holly.

Gina cleared her throat and downed the last of her tea. "I used to belong to this society, as did Maureen and Jenny, and let me tell you, those two did not get along. So society members would share recipes, and they took turns serving the group their vegetarian dishes. One week at one member's house, the next week at another member's. One night about a month ago, it was Maureen's turn. The members came to her house, and she served each one of them from individual dishes—those fluted dishes that look like small pie pans with high sides. What are they?" Gina's hands formed a circular shape.

"Ramekins?" I said.

"Ramekins. So everyone gets their own separate ramekin. And everyone but Jenny gets vegetarian stew with vegetables and seitan."

"Seitan?" Julia said.

"They call it wheat meat," Gina said. "It mimics meat."

Julia looked as though she'd just taken a bite of lemon.

"So instead of seitan, Maureen serves Jenny vegetables and *beef*. And while Jenny's eating it, she keeps saying, 'Oh my word, Maureen, this is so good! You'd never know this wasn't meat!' And Maureen just smiles away, and we're all

38

thinking the stew isn't *that* good, but Maureen is so proud and Jenny is loving it, so why spoil the night?"

I couldn't help but laugh, though I knew the story couldn't have been very funny to a serious vegetarian, and honestly, it made Maureen out to be a bit of a crazy person.

"Finally, Maureen tells Jenny she's eating beef," Gina continued. "Well, you would have thought she'd just been told she'd eaten a diseased rattlesnake. She lost it and threw the ramekin at Maureen. It hit the wall, broke, and what little was left of the stew splattered all over the place. Then Jenny started throwing the other ramekins."

"My word," Julia said.

"Good grief," I added. "Such drama." So Jenny was a bit of a crazy person too.

"Vegetarians are serious about what they put in their mouths," Gina said. "None of us liked what Maureen did. Although, for crying out loud, it was beef, not rat."

Julia made another lemon-eating face.

"Do you think Jenny was angry enough to kill Maureen over beef?"

"With Jenny, I don't think it was the beef so much as the nastiness of what Maureen did. The disrespect of it, and how she was singled out."

"I see," I said with a nod. "So why did Maureen target Jenny?"

"That's a good question. I don't know, but they were at each other's throats from the day Maureen joined the society."

"Are you still a member?"

"No, there's enough friction in life without encountering it at a vegetarian dinner. I quit. I have plenty of my own vegetarian recipes. Anyway, it was getting harder for me to visit other people's homes." She patted her cane. "I get plenty of social life sitting on this porch. I hear everything worth hearing."

"Is Tyler Hannaford a vegetarian?" I asked.

"Not that I know of, but I think he was just as angry at Maureen as Jenny was."

"So why were they on the same team for the scavenger hunt? Jenny, Tyler, Olivia—none of them liked Maureen."

"That's another good question. Jenny and Tyler work downtown, but they don't own a business, like Olivia does and Maureen did." With the help of her cane, Gina began to work her way to the edge of her seat, inch by laborious inch. "Ladies, these bones are getting chilled and I need to lie down for a while."

I stood. "Can I help?"

"If you don't mind me using you like a rope. Once I'm up, I'm fine." She stuck out her hand, and I took hold and pulled. Pain swept across Gina's face, and she let go with a breathy grunt. "It's my hips," she said, balancing herself with her cane. "My legs aren't bad at all."

My heart hurt for her. She was only in her fifties. Where would she be a decade from now?

Halfway to her screen door, Gina halted and looked back to me. "Don't leave Maureen's husband out of your investigation. Kirk Nicholson had as much reason to kill her as anyone else. She was soaking him in a divorce."

CHAPTER 5

After talking to Gina, my list of suspects in the murder of Maureen Nicholson grew, and it now included her husband, Kirk. Despite Jenny Hannaford's explosive anger during the Night of the Ramekins, I figured a messy divorce was a more likely cause of murder. I wondered if Gilroy had already talked to Kirk—or even discovered where he was, considering the man had told Olivia he was leaving town. He obviously didn't want to be found.

I dropped Julia off at her house and headed back downtown. If I was going to help Holly, I'd have to ask some serious, prying questions of all the suspects, not just nibble around the edges. My first stop was Justin Miller's steakhouse. It was almost noon, a time when the Porter Grill should have been packed, but I counted only a dozen or so people when I entered the front door. Had Maureen's call to the Health Department taken such a toll on his business?

I asked the restaurant receptionist, a woman at risk of losing her job if this was the steakhouse's typical lunchtime crowd, to tell Justin I'd like to speak to him, and while I waited, I formulated a quick plan. He was Holly's friend, and they'd both suffered at the hands of Maureen, so I'd start off by telling him I was trying to help her.

With a smile on his face—that was a good sign—Justin approached me, hand extended. "Rachel Stowe?" he asked as he shook my hand. He was a friendly looking man, but having been burned on friendly appearances before, I filed that away as irrelevant. He was in his early forties, I thought, wore wire-rimmed glasses, and sported a short-cropped salt-and-pepper goatee, which somewhat offset the starkness of his fashionably shaved head.

"Justin, thanks for taking the time to talk to me. I'm Holly Kavanagh's friend."

He nodded in recognition. "She's talked about you before—all good. Why don't we take that corner booth?"

I followed him to a private two-seater booth, as far from the front door as the seating could go, I noticed. He swung around me and directed me to one side of the booth, and then took the seat facing the window, which I suspected was the point of his maneuver.

"What can I help you with?" he said.

"I hope you don't mind me asking about the night of the scavenger hunt. You know Holly is a suspect?"

"I heard." Justin bent to retrieve something from under the table, grumbled, and came back up with a soiled napkin. "Imagine Holly killing someone."

"Her son, Caleb, is getting harassed at school."

"Kids, huh? So what do you want to know? I wasn't at the scavenger hunt, I was here. Monday's a big night."

"Okay, well, can you tell me more about Maureen's false report to the Health Department?"

Justin bristled.

"She did something similar to Holly by claiming that Holly's Sweets failed a department inspection."

"Yeah, she did. A rumor like that gets around fast. Doesn't matter what a lie it is. Maureen was a business owner—not for long, but still an owner. She knew reputation is important in the food industry."

"Then why would she do that to you?"

"I don't know."

Justin sniffed and gave his lower lip a chew—two undeniable tells. He was lying. He knew very well why Maureen had targeted him.

"You're not her competition, Holly is. It doesn't make sense."

"Maureen Nicholson was a one-woman wrecking crew," he said, scratching his chin. "She didn't need a logical reason."

I was becoming convinced that Justin was hiding something. He knew far more than he was letting on. But I wasn't going to get anywhere by pressing him on the same subject. That would only end in him throwing me out of his restaurant. I decided to approach him from another direction. "I heard Maureen cheated in this year's pumpkin contest."

Justin gave a sharp laugh and immediately relaxed. "That's what I'm talking about. She *had* to win that contest. I heard she hired someone and claimed the carving as her own. I don't mind losing, but I do mind losing to a cheater."

"Before that, you won two years in a row."

"Working in a restaurant, you get good with a knife."

We fell silent, leaving his words to hang in the air.

"That's not what I meant," he said after a moment.

"I know that," I said, trying to reassure him. "You carve radish roses, fillet delicate fish, slice vegetables paper thin—right?"

"Exactly right. It takes years to learn the craft."

"And Maureen tried to ruin you with one quick phone call."

Justin instantly got the gist of what I was saying.

43

"Yeah, but I didn't kill her. Ask anyone—I was here all night." His eyes shot to the window and his countenance brightened. "Here come Tyler and Jenny. They'll tell you. I was on their team last year, but I wasn't last night."

I looked to my right just as the Hannafords entered the restaurant. Justin slid out from the booth and waved them over. Perfect. Now I could ask Jenny about the ramekin tossing.

"Tyler, Jenny, this is Rachel Stowe, a friend of Holly's."

"We've met," Tyler said, flashing a lopsided grin. His brown hair, a little on the thin side, looked like it had been cut with blunt scissors and a bowl, and for a man in his late thirties or maybe as old as forty, he was a little soft around the middle. Not that I was in a position to criticize soft middles.

Jenny took Justin's seat in the booth, announced that she and Tyler were here for lunch, and then asked me, in a butter-wouldn't-melt way, how "poor Holly" was doing.

"She's absolutely fine," I said. I was lying, but I knew if I told Jenny that Holly was mortified and worried about her son, that information would soon make the gossip rounds.

"I'm glad to hear it," Jenny said. She leaned forward and spoke in a this-is-confidential tone. "She had nothing to do with this. Someone put that flash drive in her backpack."

"I figured as much."

"Have they found out whose blood it was?" she asked.

"Not that I know of." Now it was my turn to lean forward. "Can I ask you a question? I'm trying to help Holly out."

"Of course, of course."

Justin remained standing, but Tyler motioned for Jenny to move over and then sat on the edge of the cushioned booth seat, all ears. "Justin, grab a chair," he said.

Justin waved him off.

"I'm getting the impression that Maureen Nicholson wasn't a popular woman," I said.

Jenny snorted.

"Can I ask you why she was on Team Main Street with you, Tyler, and Olivia?"

"Oh, that's easy," Jenny said. She lifted a hand to smooth an unruly lock of blonde hair and the narrow silver bangles on her wrist jangled. "She asked to join us."

"That's it?"

"Her business was a little off the beaten track, but in a sense she was still a Main Streeter. We couldn't turn her down. Not without suffering for it, anyway."

"That's for sure," Justin said. He nodded gravely and plucked at his goatee. "Man oh man, she would've made all of us pay."

Here before me were three adults, in their late thirties to early forties, yet when faced with a mere woman, they cowed like frightened children. It made no sense. "Why did you all put up with her?"

Tyler swiveled a little in his seat to face me directly. "I'm the manager of the Spruce Tavern downtown. You know what Maureen said to me? She said, 'It would be a shame for you to lose your food license.' This is two weeks after I started the job. Two weeks." He palmed back his wispy bangs. "What kind of person says that?"

"Was she threatening you?"

"Was she . . . ?" Tyler shook his head. "You obviously never met her."

45

"She didn't make threats, she announced her plans," Jenny added.

"You could have banded together and made it clear she couldn't bully you," I said.

"Could have, should have," Jenny said. "None of us handled her very well, I admit that."

"It was easier to let her win," Tyler said.

"And avoid her whenever possible," Justin said. "It's like when you're a kid at school. Someone bullies you, and at first you try to get along with the bully. That doesn't work, so you fight back. But soon you realize that doesn't work either. Maureen was like that. Always a kid at school, always bullying. You could only appease her temporarily, not stop her."

"But someone stopped her," I said. "Was she friendly with anyone in town?" I glanced from Justin to Tyler to Jenny. They shook their heads.

"Not that I know of," Jenny said. "She didn't even get along with her husband."

"She must have been very lonely," I said. By all accounts Maureen was a scheming, vindictive woman, but I felt a twinge of pity for her. I couldn't imagine the isolation she must have felt, even though it was of her own making. She had lived in a beautiful town, full of potential friends on every corner, yet she'd chosen to make a pariah of herself.

"She didn't have to be," Jenny said.

"Well . . . ," Tyler said. He slapped his knees and made a move to stand up. "Another booth, I think."

"Just one more question," I said.

"Does Chief Gilroy know you're playing private detective?" Tyler said. There was a bit of a twinkle in his brown eyes, but his tone wasn't entirely lighthearted.

"I'm sure he does." I wasn't *playing* at anything, I wanted to say, but with one important question left to go, I didn't want to antagonize him. "On the night of the scavenger hunt, you and Jenny left witch hats with a riddle on them in Gina Peeler's yard."

"Sure, I remember," Jenny said. "We also put the clue leading to the hats at the first checkpoint, where Julia Foster was."

"But Gina wasn't part of the hunt. No one asked her permission."

"Really?" Tyler said. "Homeowners have to sign up for the hunt. You can't just plant scavenger finds in their yards."

"That's what I thought," I said.

"We were told she was part of the hunt," Jenny said.

Tyler nodded vigorously. "Olivia said so. She told us the clues for Gina's yard had been left out by accident and asked if we would mind taking them there and putting the clue leading to them at the first checkpoint. We thought it was funny that Olivia would know where any clue was, or that we were allowed to plant a clue, since we were playing, but there you are."

"We saw Gina at the window when we were hiding the witch hats, and she never said anything to us," Jenny said.

"There must have been a misunderstanding," Tyler said. "Gina might have forgotten she signed up."

"I don't think so," I said. "The clue that led people to her house was cruel. It said, 'Put the spider in your bag, then leave this place to see the hag.' Gina was the hag."

"No, no, no," Tyler said, holding up a hand. "The hag was a stuffed witch on a porch on the same block. No way would we make it Gina Peeler."

"Folks, I've got to go," Justin said, glancing anxiously

47

toward the kitchen. Beads of sweat had formed on his brow. "I've got a chef situation today. Tyler, Jenny, good to see you. Rachel, nice to meet you."

Justin took off and disappeared through a swinging door on the far side of the restaurant. Either he truly had a chef situation, whatever that was, or my questions were making him uneasy. Tyler and Jenny had probably had enough of me too, but I wasn't finished with them.

"How do you know the witch on the porch was the hag?" I asked.

"Because we went there and found the next scavenger clue," Jenny said, her tone suggesting a postscript: *You idiot.*

"Rubber snakes," Tyler added.

Jenny's eyes narrowed. "Where did you and Holly go after Julia Foster's body?"

"To Gina's," I replied. "By the time we got there, Gina had already been asked a few times if she was the hag in the third clue."

Tyler and his wife exchanged skeptical looks.

"So Julia was checkpoint one," I said, counting off on my fingers, "the stuffed witch on the porch was checkpoint two. Which checkpoint was Gina's? How far down on the list was it?"

"I don't know," Jenny said. "We never got there. We saw everyone running down the street and went to find out what was happening."

Feeling I'd overstayed my welcome, I thanked the Hannafords and slid out of the booth. "Jenny, I heard you were a vegetarian."

"Yes?"

"This is a steakhouse."

"Justin has some delicious vegetarian dishes on his

menu."

I left the Porter Grill and headed for my car. Thunder rolled in the distance. Dark clouds had moved in, chasing away the crisp October sunshine. We were in for a storm.

Just as I shut the door of my Forester, the raindrops began, splashing large and heavy on the windshield. Someone was lying. Someone or nearly everyone. Had I just added another suspect to my growing list? Olivia was already on it. I didn't trust her. But now I wondered if Gina had lied to me about the hag clue. And was Gina Peeler, by all appearances hardly able to move, capable of murder?

CHAPTER 6

I drove west down Main Street, parked a block up from the Juniper Grove Police Station, and sat in my car, waiting for the storm to pass. Chief Gilroy was going to hear from someone that I'd questioned Justin and the Hannafords, so why not tell him myself? He had no right to stop me, I told myself, and maybe I could scrape up a few clues by talking to him. And I could put in a good word for Holly. Gilroy had to know that Holly was innocent. And he needed to know that the longer he waited to declare her innocence, the more miserable he was making her son's life.

My stomach growled, and it took every ounce of my wavering willpower not to dash to Holly's Sweets for a cream puff before seeing Gilroy—if he was even at the station. My willpower stabilized when I recalled running into him a few weeks back, blueberry jelly from a donut dripping down the front of my shirt. I'd looked an absolute slob. Was that why he'd been avoiding me?

After he had rescued me—well, kind of rescued me—from a killer in September and taken me to the station for my statement, he'd seemed interested. In *me*. Or at least that's how I had wanted to read his words and expressions. Afterward, I imagined him asking me out. Taking his sweet time to do it, but doing it. I pictured getting lost in his icy blue eyes.

I shook my head to dispel all thoughts of any future with James Gilroy. With Julia's encouragement—insistence, really—I was at least leaving my ex-fiance in the distant past. If twelve years can be called distant. Brent was his name. He'd asked me to marry him and then left without a word a week before the wedding. For a week after that, I was terrified that something dreadful had happened to him. Then a friend of a friend had spotted him in a bar in Denver, alive, well, and happy. The love of my life hadn't cared enough to tell me he no longer wanted to marry me. The light went out of my life, and five years later, still mourning him, I'd moved to Boston.

"Enough," I said aloud. I looked to the windshield. The rain had eased enough for me to make a dash down the sidewalk without getting soaked. I got out and darted for the police station.

An overworked Officer Underhill, stacks of folders at both elbows, greeted me with a grimace as I walked in. "The chief is in his office," he said. "Go ahead."

"How did you know I wanted to talk to him?"

"He probably wants to talk to you."

I started for Gilroy's door but pivoted back. "Why?"

"You're talking to people aren't you?"

"Has anyone complained?"

"Not that I know of."

Underhill went back to his work. Whatever he was doing, it seemed to require a deeply furrowed brow. The department was sorely in need of a third officer, but Gilroy hadn't as yet hired one. And now there was a murder to contend with. The chief needed to be out on the streets doing his job, I thought, not sitting behind a desk.

I covered the short trip from the front desk to Gilroy's

office in two seconds and knocked on his open door.

"Yes?" he said, slowly looking up from a sheet of paper that had his rapt attention.

"Have you got a moment?"

"Sure." He gestured toward a chair, dropped the paper, and leaned back in his seat. "What can I do for you?"

He was wearing his standard uniform—shirt, suit jacket, no tie. Probably jeans too. Very un-Boston, and I liked it. "Before you hear anything from anyone else, I wanted to tell you that I've talked to a few people about the night of the scavenger hunt."

"That's not surprising."

"I'm trying to help Holly. Her son is getting bullied at school, and kids are calling her a murderer."

"Kids will do stuff like that. There's nothing much you can do about it."

"Clearing her of murder would be a start."

Gilroy's dark eyebrows went up. "She hasn't been charged."

"Olivia Seitz screamed about blood when you found that flash drive. News probably made the gossip circuit in town within an hour. Why do you think Caleb's classmates called his mom a murderer?"

He sat straight and leaned his forearms on his desk. "I haven't charged her, Miss Stowe, and—"

"Rachel. Remember?"

"Rachel. And I don't foresee charging her, at least not now."

I was appalled. I wanted him to say he would never charge her, period. That to do so would be absurd. "Would you actually charge her?"

"With what I have now? No."

"You've known Holly for years."

"Who I know and don't know has nothing to do with it."

He folded his hands atop the sheet of paper he'd examined earlier, looking every bit the in-control police chief. *Maddening*. The man was a monotone, one-syllable, maddening man, and every time I looked into his eyes or saw the slight wave of his dark hair, I melted. And now his hands. "This is ridiculous."

"What is?"

I hadn't meant to say that aloud. I recovered quickly. "Someone put that flash drive in her backpack."

"That's a fair assumption."

My jaw dropped. "So you know it was a plant? Why aren't you telling people that?"

"That's not my job, Rachel. Not without proof. And it's not your job to investigate."

"I have every right."

"To some extent."

"Was there anything on the flash drive?"

"I can't talk about that either."

"Was the blood on the flash drive Maureen's?"

"I can't talk about that either."

"Is that the report on it?" I pointed at the sheet of paper.

"I can't discuss the case."

"Come on, Holly's my friend."

"Rachel, it's been less than twenty-four hours. Give it time."

"Would you like to hear what I found out?"

I thought I saw a faint smile on his face.

"Sure," he said.

I told Gilroy everything Gina and the Hannafords had

told me about the "hag" clue, including that Olivia had asked the Hannafords to place the witch hats in Gina's yard. He listened with interest, and when I stopped talking, he wrote a note on a scrap of paper and set it to the side. Then he stood and stretched his back, something I'd seen him do before and something I did after long periods of time writing at my desk. But he was trim and I was . . . well, I wasn't.

"Anything else?" he asked.

Not a single word of thanks. I'd meddled again, encroached on his territory. "No, that's it. Thanks for your time."

As I strode for the front door, Underhill, still up to his elbow in folders, gave me a quizzical look. I halted and gave him one back. "What is it?" I asked.

"Do you two . . . ?" he said softly, making a back-and-forth motion with one hand.

"What?"

He leaned forward, keeping his voice low. "I mean, are you two, you know, seeing each other?"

I reared back. "Why do you ask that?"

"Because he doesn't put up with stuff like that from anyone else."

"Oh." Hearing a rustle from Gilroy's office, I raced for the door. I grabbed the handle, but instead of making a smart exit, I glanced over my shoulder. Gilroy was approaching Underhill. He gave me a nod, and my hand slipped. I grabbed the door handle again, shot a smile over my shoulder, and nearly flung myself outside.

Mortified, I made for my car—wisely without a backward glance. Underhill's words played over in my mind. *He doesn't put up with stuff like that from anyone else.* My emotions were a strange mixture of confused, giddy, and unbelieving. Unbelieving because I felt I was getting ahead of myself, sensing something that wasn't there. Chief Gilroy acted like Chief Gilroy in front of me—the same way he acted with everyone else. Confident, polite, and faintly put out. But if Underhill wasn't imagining things, what did that mean? And what, precisely, was "stuff like that"? Were the citizens of Juniper Grove not allowed to question their police chief?

The storm still hovered overhead, but it had lost its intensity. I rolled down my window a couple inches, reveling in the scent of wet bark on the rain-blackened trees, the sound of tires *shooshing* on the glistening pavement. Ahead, the foothills were shrouded in low clouds. The rain was going to stick around for a while.

I started the engine, determined to stay focused on Maureen Nicholson's murder and forget about the Door Handle Episode. Gilroy hadn't expressed a strong objection to my investigation, so I was going to take that as a green light and forge ahead. It was time to call a meeting of the Juniper Grove Mystery Gang, Holly's name for our little crew of oddball detectives: me, a single woman in her forties; Julia, a widow in her sixties; and Holly, a married woman in her thirties. With our different perspectives, we made a great team.

I glanced in my rearview mirror, ready to pull from the curb, but I stopped when I saw Justin Miller on the sidewalk, engaged in what appeared to be an argument with another man. The subtle kind of argument in which the participants were furious but, finding themselves in public, tried not to show it too much. I angled in my seat for a better look out the back window. The other man was perhaps a little older than Justin, with a full head of brown hair. Watching him in profile, it was clear that his distinguishing feature was an exceptionally prominent nose. He matched perfectly Olivia's description of Kirk Nicholson: mid-forties, brown hair, big nose.

But why was Justin arguing with the recently bereaved Kirk? I shut off my car, got out, and headed toward them as they continued to argue. I was on my way to the bakery, I'd say, and just happened to run into them. I needed a dessert for tonight anyway.

I slowed as I neared them. I smiled at Justin and turned to the other man. "Kirk Nicholson?"

He glowered at me.

"My name is Rachel Stowe. I was so sorry to hear about your wife."

"Oh, right. Thank you."

"Like a lot of people, I was on the scavenger hunt last night."

"Maureen enjoyed events like that. I didn't care for them. Did you know my wife?"

"No, I didn't, but some of my friends did."

"Maureen didn't have a lot of friends. She had a reputation for bullying."

What could I say? By now I'd heard enough about Maureen Nicholson to know that was true, but I wasn't about to agree with Kirk that his wife was probably the most unlikeable person in Juniper Grove.

"I'm sorry," I mumbled.

"I guess she paid the price," Kirk said. "She played with fire and got burnt."

"No one deserves to be murdered," I said.

Justin grunted and reached up to massage the back of his neck with his hand.

"Comment, Justin?" Kirk said.

"None at all, Kirk," Justin said, glaring at his combatant. With that he marched back into the Porter Grill.

Kirk waited until Justin disappeared into the restaurant before speaking. "Well, Rachel, I think there's a difference between deserving something and suffering the natural consequences of your actions."

Now was my chance to ask about the Night of the Ramekins. It was clear that Kirk wasn't that broken up about his wife's death, which made broaching the subject easier. "Actions like feeding Jenny Hannaford beef at a vegetarian dinner?"

Kirk let go with a single, harsh laugh. "You heard about that, did you? Maureen shouldn't have done it, but do you know what Jenny did in response?"

"Yes, I heard."

"So tell me, who was more out of control? Jenny or my wife?" He wearily rubbed his eyes. "I'm sorry. Maybe both of them were. But it was never about beef and vegetarians. It was about the Juniper Grove Development Association and the supermarket."

"What supermarket?"

"It's not surprising you haven't heard about it. The association killed the idea so it couldn't come to a vote. Half the members in the association wanted to allow a supermarket to be built, half didn't. My wife wanted it, Jenny Hannaford and Olivia Seitz didn't. And they were all running for president of the association. You're searching for Maureen's killer, right?"

How did he know? I hesitated to answer.

"News gets around fast in this town. You go ahead and try to find out, with my blessing. It's not a secret that

Maureen and I weren't getting along. We were getting a divorce, in fact. Maybe she didn't deserve to have friends, but she didn't deserve to be murdered. If you're serious about finding her killer, forget about beef and start with the development association."

CHAPTER 7

After we had cleared the dinner dishes from my table and set them in the sink, I pulled the pink Holly's Sweets box from my fridge. Four luscious cream puffs—one for me, Holly, and Julia, and the fourth for my breakfast tomorrow. I'd been two weeks without the best pastry in Colorado, and I was going to make up for it.

"Let's go upstairs to my office," I said, cradling the box.

"Have you got your corkboard crime scene laid out?" Julia asked, a twinkle in her eye.

"As a matter of fact, I do."

Holly, eager to get going, led us up my creaking wooden staircase and down the hall to the small bedroom where I plotted and wrote my mystery novels. My desk faced a giant corkboard, now covered with index cards bearing the suspects' names, lists of motives and opportunities, and, along the bottom of the board, a time line fashioned from more index cards.

"Very impressive," Holly said, untying the string from the pastry box.

"There are so many details to this case that I think if we can see everything at a glance, we may get a better idea of what happened."

"I'm a *case* now," Holly said forlornly. She handed me

59

and then Julia a cream puff.

"You're our friend," I said. "This"—I pointed at the board—"is the case, not you. You're only involved because someone put that flash drive in your backpack."

"And we're going to set things right," Julia said. "So don't you worry."

I stopped to indulge in a bite of cream puff, rolling my eyes as I tasted it and the cream filling oozed. "I don't know how you do it," I said to Holly. "This is not your ordinary cream puff."

Holly grinned. "A lot of people don't get the pastry right. They make it too heavy when it's supposed to be airy."

"This pastry is like a cloud."

"You have to get the cream right too, of course."

"Ladies," Julia said, licking filling from the corner of her mouth, "enough food talk. Let's get to work."

For the next ten minutes I went over what I'd learned—from Chief Gilroy, Justin Miller, and the Hannafords—and recapped for Holly what Julia and I had heard from Gina. Then I concentrated on Kirk Nicholson and his suggestion that the Juniper Grove Development Association and doomed supermarket idea was at the heart of his wife's murder.

"Have either of you heard of this group?" I asked.

"Oh sure," Holly said. "All the merchants have."

"What political power do they have?"

"Not much, except that they can put the brakes on things like that supermarket before the plans even get to the mayor and Board of Trustees."

"I would have liked a supermarket," I said, a little miffed that I'd never even heard it was being considered. "I get tired of driving to Loveland or Fort Collins when I need more than a few pieces of fruit."

"A lot of association members were afraid of traffic issues," Holly said.

I sat on the edge of my desk. "There are twelve hundred people in Juniper Grove. How bad can traffic get?"

Holly shrugged. "I don't understand it either. And it's not as if a supermarket would attract out-of-towners. They have their own supermarkets."

"It's something to consider," I said, looking back to the board. "The supermarket was doomed, but Maureen, Olivia, and Jenny were still running for president of the association. When was the vote going to take place?"

"Tomorrow," Holly replied.

"Lucky timing for Olivia and Jenny, huh?"

"The meeting's tomorrow morning and it's open to the public. Want to go?"

"You bet I do. Did Maureen have a chance of winning?"

"Believe it or not, she was the front-runner with the other members. She had contacts up and down the Front Range and she was a go-getter. They needed her energy. Now I think it's a toss-up between Olivia and Jenny."

"Would either of them murder just to be president of the association?" Julia asked. "I can't buy that."

"I'm not sure I do either," I said. "Though it's interesting that Jenny didn't mention the upcoming vote when I talked to her. And speaking of contests . . ." I strode to the board and tapped my list of motives. "There's no more ridiculous motivation than Maureen winning the pumpkin-carving contest and cheating Justin Miller out of first place."

"Justin felt entitled to win," Julia said.

I twisted back to Holly. "How's the Porter Grill doing?

When I talked to Justin there were maybe a dozen customers, and it was noon."

"The Porter Grill used to be a steak-and-potatoes place," Holly said. "Great rustic food. But a few weeks back he changed the menu, and now a lot of what he serves isn't his strong suit. It's still a good restaurant—it's run well, it's clean—but he's no longer catering to the same clientele. A restaurant can only have so many entrees on its menu. Too many and it's chaos in the kitchen. So in order to make room on his new menu, he had to stop serving some of his most popular entrees. Instead of porterhouse steak, he serves Thai noodle salad."

"Vegetarian dishes," I said.

"There are two small restaurants in Juniper Grove that do that kind of food, and do it better. Justin lost half his customers, but he's so stubborn."

"Why would a man sabotage his own business?" I said. Immediately I thought of Jenny. What if Jenny and Justin were having an affair? It might be reason enough for Justin to change his menu. I'd seen both men and women change like chameleons to cater to the new loves in their lives. But to mention the possibility to Holly and Julia would be adding my own gossip to the already hefty gossip mill. I decided to keep the idea to myself until I had confirmation.

Holly stepped closer to the board and examined my list of motives. "Maureen went after Justin's restaurant at a bad time for him. Calling the Health Department, making his customers think he was running a dirty kitchen. He's been exhausted lately. I can see it in his face."

"Is he capable of murder?" Julia asked.

"To watch your livelihood disappear, your hopes and dreams fade?" Holly turned back. "A few years ago I might have said no."

I was about to ask her about her own Maureen-instigated Health Department incident, but I thought better of it. For whatever reason, she hadn't told me that Maureen had spread rumors about Holly's Sweets failing a department inspection, and I had to respect that. My curiosity wasn't sufficient justification for invading her privacy.

"My money's on Olivia Seitz," Julia said.

"What about her husband, Eric?" Holly asked.

"He never left his porch," Julia said. "I heard him all night, trying to get the other teams to stop what they were doing and have some cider."

"Even if he had left," I said, "he couldn't have made it from his front porch to more than three blocks away in that short period of time." Now that I thought of it, neither could Gina have made it from her porch to a house more than two blocks away from hers. We'd talked for several minutes, and then Holly and I had left to solve the nest riddle. Two minutes later, participants were texting each other about a second body. I was relieved by the thought and felt foolish for not having considered it earlier.

I directed Holly and Julia's attention to my index-card time line. "I think the killer was someone who passed us by early on or was already down the street from us. With each passing minute, more teams were heading up the street, so he or she acted early in the hunt and acted fast. And remember, it doesn't have to be a participant in the scavenger hunt. Kirk and Justin said they didn't play, but that doesn't mean they weren't there. Everyone thought Kirk was out of town, and Justin could have slipped away from the Porter Grill."

"My phone's buzzing," Holly said, pulling her cell

phone from her jeans pocket. While she stepped into the hall, Julia and I considered our other suspects. Julia insisted that Olivia was just the kind of cold woman to have knifed Maureen.

"Who do you suspect?" she asked.

"All of them and none of them. They each have their reasons for wanting Maureen dead. If Justin didn't kill her because she stole the first-place carving ribbon from him, he killed her for making a false report to the Health Department. If Jenny didn't kill her for feeding her beef, she killed her so she could become president of the Juniper Grove Development Association. And so on and so on."

"What would Tyler Hannaford's motive be?" she asked.

"To support Jenny?"

Looking shaken, Holly reentered the office. "Caleb's at the police station. Peter just got a call from Chief Gilroy."

"What?" I said. "Why?"

"He got into a fight downtown. He caught someone from his school writing 'Murderer' on the bakery window."

"Holly . . ."

She put up her hands. "If either of you hugs me now, I'll cry. The past two months have been a royal mess."

I stayed put. "Tell me Gilroy didn't arrest Caleb."

"He didn't, thank goodness. And he brought in the little snot who was writing on the window." She sniffed loudly. "He didn't arrest him either. He wants the parents to meet and settle things."

"That's wise," Julia said.

"Is Peter at home?" I asked.

"Yeah, he's waiting for me. I'd better go."

"Tell him we said hello and we're sorry," I called down

the stairs as she hurried for the front door.

"That's it," I said as I marched back into my office. "This has got to stop. The Kavanaghs shouldn't have to put up with this."

"I hope Chief Gilroy sentences that boy to washing the bakery window for six months."

I chuckled. Window washing as a sentence was as medieval as my sweet neighbor got. "I thought you wanted the parents to settle it."

"I wouldn't mind if the chief gave his own punishment for added measure."

I walked to the bedroom's single window, pushed back the cotton drapes, and looked out across the street, where Holly and Peter were getting into their car for what was sure to be a miserable trip to and from the police station. Holly was right. The past two months had been a royal mess for her. In September a vandal had broken into her bakery, destroying everything she'd baked for the Farmers' Market Festival, and now Gilroy had taken in her thirteen-year-old son and some people in town suspected her of murder.

If only she hadn't left her backpack by the picket fence. How easy it had been for the killer to stroll by and drop the drive inside the open pocket. Trying to recall the faces of everyone I saw that night, all of us corralled into a neighbor's yard, was a pointless exercise. I could only remember a few. But I was fairly certain that Holly's backpack had been chosen at random—the open pocket presenting the killer with an opportunity—and there was some comfort in that. She hadn't been targeted, she'd been unlucky.

My guess was that Gilroy hadn't found anything on the flash drive. But there didn't need to be anything on it. All the killer had to do was use the promise of it, the supposed information it held, to lure Maureen to her death. Give her a riddle, draw her in. No wonder she hadn't stayed with her team. She wasn't there for the hunt, she was there for the promise of that bright blue drive. Did the killer strike when she bent to pick it up? Or wait until she stood erect, her attention riveted to it?

Whichever way it happened, that drive had done double duty, as both a lure for Maureen and a device to implicate someone else and throw Gilroy off the trail.

CHAPTER 8

Understandably, Holly wasn't in a mood to go the Juniper Grove Development Association meeting the next morning, but Julia wanted to go and act as another pair of eyes. We both knew there was a good chance Maureen's killer would be in attendance, since the entire town had been invited—the association, interested business owners, and the general public. The meeting was wisely being held in the Board of Trustee's boardroom, the largest space in Town Hall, but still the place was packed when Julia and I arrived. Every seat had been taken, though judging by the number of chairs crammed into the room, someone had scoured Town Hall for extra seating. We ended up standing at the back, along with thirty other people.

I scanned the room for familiar faces, my eyes immediately falling on Olivia Seitz and Jenny Hannaford, both of them sitting at a long conference table at the head of the room. On either side of them were several more people. I didn't recognize any of them.

"Are those eight people the association members?" I asked Julia, nodding at the table.

"I imagine so," she said. "I've never been to one of these meetings. I had no idea they were so popular."

Continuing to search the room, I saw Tyler Hannaford in a seat near the front of the room, gazing adoringly at his wife, and Justin Miller one row of seats behind him. I scoured the room for Eric Seitz and finally found him, standing with arms folded, in the northwest corner of the room near a second exit door.

Then I caught sight of Chief Gilroy. He was sitting in a folding chair along the west wall, his elbows on his knees, his hands folded, his right foot tapping a rhythm. I'd never noticed before, but he was wearing cowboy boots—or at least they looked like cowboy boots, since most of the boots were hidden by his jeans legs. There was no turquoise stitching on the toes, nothing fancy. Just plain brown boots. Very un-Boston. And I liked it.

I leaned sideways and whispered to Julia, "All our suspects are here."

"Gathered in one place. How opportune."

I chuckled. "I wonder how contentious this election will be."

"With those two women running? There's trouble ahead."

"Do the candidates give speeches?"

"I certainly hope not. My feet can't take it."

When I glanced at Gilroy again, he met my eyes and raised his chin in greeting. I smiled and looked away. In my peripheral vision I saw him stand and head my way. I mumbled under my breath.

"What was that?" Julia asked.

I mumbled again.

"Good morning, ladies," Gilroy said.

"Chief Gilroy, I didn't see you," Julia said.

"Mrs. Foster, would you like to take my seat?" He gestured toward the west wall.

Julia's hand rose to her collarbone. "Oh, how nice.

Thank you so much. It would be lovely not to stand all morning. I'm afraid they're going to make speeches."

Gilroy led her across the room to his chair, and Julia, gushing additional thanks by the looks of it, took his seat. So he was a gentleman. Thoughtful and polite. In cowboy boots. So what? I needed to focus on the task at hand. Holly and Caleb needed my help. As Gilroy headed back across the room to where I was standing, a woman at the front of the room called for order, and I resolved to keep my eyes on the audience and off Gilroy.

The chief took Julia's spot next to me just as the meeting began. Folding his arms over his chest, he stared straight ahead.

"I'm sure you've all heard of the tragic death of one of our JGDA members, Maureen Nicholson," the woman said. "While we grieve Maureen, the members decided not to delay but to go ahead with the election of a president. I think that's why we have an overflow crowd this morning."

Gentle laughter rippled across the room.

"We have two candidates," the woman continued. "Jenny Hannaford and Olivia Seitz. Jenny is the manager of Haven Art on Lilac Lane, and Olivia owns Blooms on Main Street. Now, as you know, the association has no voting power within town government, but the mayor and Juniper Grove Board of Trustees take our recommendations very seriously. In fact, most development in town begins as a recommendation from the association. With that in mind, let's hear from Jenny Hannaford first."

There was a smattering of applause as Jenny rose and walked to the microphone. So we would have to endure speeches after all.

"Ladies and gentlemen, I'll keep it short. We all need

to get out of here and get to that second cup of coffee, don't we? And you don't need us prattling away up here."

Smart, I thought. *Now Olivia has to keep it short too.*

"I'm not a business owner," Jenny continued. "But then, half of the board isn't." She extended her arms to the left and right, indicating the other board members. "You may think that's a disadvantage, but I think it's an advantage. I see the business community from both sides. As a manager, I'm like an owner, responsible for sales and running the store. But I'm also in direct contact with customers, including visitors to our town. I know what they want to see and what they don't want to see. I talk to them every day. If you elect me, you'll get that experience and perspective. Thank you."

More generous applause and a few shouts of "Yes!" followed. Jenny took her seat, and Olivia rose and moved for the microphone. Wanting to gauge Gilroy's reaction to what Jenny had said, I turned my head slightly while avoiding direct eye contact. But he was no longer staring straight ahead. His arms still crossed over his chest, he seemed to be searching the room. He wasn't at the meeting out of interest, I realized. He was on the job.

"Thank you, Jenny," Olivia said, brushing back her dark bangs. "I appreciate your perspective, I really do, but I believe that as business owners, we have a unique position in town. And not only position. Owners have networks to draw on for information and support. We're intimately connected to town and state governments, even if sometimes we'd rather not be."

That brought on hearty laughs and hand claps. Now Olivia was winning the room.

"In short, as a business owner, I know how to get things

70

done, and I have the support system to do it. But just as important as knowing when to develop, I know when *not* to develop. I'll listen to owners, managers, and customers, and in the end, I'll do what's best for Juniper Grove. Thank you."

Olivia took her seat to applause I judged to be slightly more enthusiastic than Jenny's. Was her speech an affirmation of the anti-supermarket alliance? Was that how the crowd saw it? Jenny hadn't even hinted at the subject.

This time I looked directly at Gilroy, who was staring straight ahead again as we waited for the vote. "What happened to that kid who got into a fight with Caleb?" I asked.

"You'll have to ask Holly about that," he said, still staring.

"Do you know about the supermarket Maureen Nicholson wanted to bring to town?"

His pale blue eyes shifted to mine. "Sure."

"Kirk Nicholson said both Olivia and Jenny were against it."

"You talked to Kirk Nicholson?" He dropped his arms and let his hands dangle at his sides.

"He hasn't been hiding exactly, even though Maureen told people he was going to be out of town. Julia saw him coming out of an office building next to Town Hall."

"Do you have any idea how dangerous it is to question people about a murder? It's not a game like the scavenger hunt."

"That wasn't much of a game, either, and Kirk didn't kill his wife."

"You know that, do you?"

I shrugged. It wouldn't do any good to say my instincts were telling me Kirk wasn't a killer. I was pretty sure Gilroy didn't operate on instincts and didn't understand mine.

"You live alone," he said.

"So what?"

"What if someone broke in? How would you defend yourself?"

"Who's going to break in?"

"Someone you've made angry."

"I have a weapon."

"Do you know how to use it?"

The man standing next to me shoved a petulant face our way and shushed us. Gilroy returned to staring straight ahead.

"Yup, I do," I whispered.

No wonder the man had shushed us. The association had run more than halfway down the conference table, taking each member's vote. There were three votes left to go.

"Olivia Seitz," a man said. He turned to the woman on his right.

"Jenny Hannaford," the woman said. She in turn looked to her right.

"Olivia Seitz."

The audience erupted in applause, and Olivia, who must have won, grinned broadly and shook Jenny's hand. I didn't know how hard fought the campaign for president had been, but Jenny handled the loss well, giving Olivia's hand a firm shake and smiling good-naturedly.

Just as I was about to say something to Gilroy, he pulled his phone from his suit pocket, checked it, and rushed for the main exit to our right.

I'd grown used to Gilroy's sudden departures without so much as a polite goodbye, so I cut through what was left of the crowd to where Julia still sat and took the empty chair next to hers.

"I'm sorry I left you standing while I got to sit," she said, "but I noticed you had a chance to talk to Chief Gilroy." She nudged me with her elbow. She was doing more and more nudging these days, and I was growing less and less fond of it.

"Julia, I don't think you grasp the content of my conversations with Gilroy."

"I also noticed he made a point of standing next to you."

"I'm going to record the next conversation I have with him on my phone, and I'll play it back to you."

Julia was aghast. "You wouldn't do that."

"I'd consider it if it would make my point for me. Come on, let's get out of here."

On the sidewalk outside Town Hall, I searched the lingering crowd for Kirk Nicholson, though I knew it was unlikely he'd shown up. We'd left Olivia and Eric Seitz inside, probably celebrating, and Jenny and Tyler Hannaford too, probably commiserating. Though the meeting and vote hadn't appeared to be acrimonious, I had sensed undercurrents of resentment between the couples. Justin Miller had made a point of looking neutral, neither clapping nor cheering, but I would have bet he was rooting for Jenny.

"Julia, where's the office building you saw Kirk Nicholson coming out of Monday afternoon?"

"Right there," Julia said, leading me ten feet up the sidewalk. "This is the door. I'm positive."

It was a typical-looking Juniper Grove office building, limestone on the outside and the occupants' names in white lettering on the glass entrance door. "Look at this. An architect, a designer, a chiropractic office, and a law firm.

That explains why Kirk was here. He's getting a divorce and was seeing his lawyer. Maybe he signed the final papers."

"I'll bet you're right. And he didn't want anyone to know."

"He didn't think it was anyone else's business. But he must have known someone would see him."

"It's peculiar timing, though. Signing divorce papers on the day Maureen was murdered."

"Why would he bother to sign the papers and then kill his wife hours later? That's even more peculiar. Anyway, we're speculating. We don't know that he signed anything while he was here, and I don't think he hated his wife. I think he hated his marriage."

Julia replied with a nod. It was a sentiment she understood. The last years of her marriage to George Foster had been dry and cold, and when he'd deserted her after stealing a small fortune from a local bank, an unbreachable wall had formed between them. But she had never hated him.

"I still don't know why Kirk and Justin were arguing on the sidewalk outside the Porter Grill," I said.

"Did you hear the mayor and Town Board canceled Halloween? It was in the *Juniper Grove Post* this morning."

The new and vastly improved *Post*, I thought, now that its scandal-mongering editor was gone. "The kids aren't going to like that."

I saw the Town Hall door swing wide. Justin and the Hannafords strolled out of the building and onto the sidewalk, pausing there to chat for a moment. Before they parted, Justin and Tyler shook hands, and then Jenny wrapped her arms around Justin and held him tightly, finally releasing him with a pat on his back.

CHAPTER 9

I had wondered if Justin Miller and Jenny Hannaford were having an affair, and if that was why Justin had changed the menu at the Porter Grill, but no longer. Whatever was going on between the two, it was in full sight of Tyler Hannaford, and middle-aged paunch or not, he didn't strike me as a man who would sit still for his wife flaunting her love for another man right in front of him. But it went beyond that. Justin and Jenny's embrace, though more than casual, had the appearance of deep friendship, not passionate love.

Julia and I decided to make a stop at Maureen's old shop, Coffee and Cakes, to see if it was still open. And if it was, who was running it. The little drive-through was northwest of downtown, on Cedar Avenue, a two-lane road that led to parks and recreation areas in town and then into the foothills, where it became a county road. A brilliant location for a drive-through.

It being the lone building on a straight stretch of the avenue, painted sky blue to boot, we had no trouble finding it. But there wasn't a drive-through customer in sight, and when we drove up to the order window, it became clear that Coffee and Cakes had closed.

"Such a shame," Julia said. "Didn't she have any employees?"

"I'm sure she did, but who would pay them now that

75

she's gone? If Kirk didn't have a financial interest in the shop or his name wasn't on the property, he wouldn't try to keep it open. It's a smart place to put a food establishment, though." I drove around the building again, then pulled to the side of the circular drive that wove around it, parked, and got out.

"I don't understand why Maureen thought Holly and Justin were threats to her," I said as Julia joined me. "Her customer base couldn't have been theirs. Their places are completely different."

"I agree. This is for people who want a quick cup of coffee and a pastry before driving to the parks or mountains. No one else lives or works around here."

The sky was a soft gray broken by patches of blue, and the clouds still tufts of white drifting by, but I could smell rain on the air. "It's going to rain again," I said. "A storm's coming. Do you smell that?"

"I do. Let's get in the car."

I stood for a minute longer, taking in the sweet scent. This part of Cedar Avenue was on a low ridge, and from my vantage point, I could see a shallow valley not far below us, studded with trees that were half bare and half a brilliant autumn gold. *Thank you, God.* How could I not be grateful for a sight like that? I was fortunate to live here. Fortunate to be standing in that place, not in a big-city office. Fortunate to be dressed in jeans and hiking shoes rather than the dressy work clothes I loathed.

I could have breathed it all in for at least another hour, but I was keeping Julia waiting—she had a day of pumpkin pie baking ahead of her at home—and I had plans to head downtown again and pay a visit to Blooms, Olivia Seitz's store. Congratulations on her win, and a couple questions about the scavenger hunt, were in order. I climbed back into my Forester as thunder began to rumble in the distance.

We were one step ahead of the incoming rain as we drove east into town, but by the time I'd pulled away from Julia's house, the storm had caught up with me and a cold, hard rain was beating against the windshield. Downtown, I parked two shops down from Blooms. I reached back and snagged my umbrella from the passenger seat behind me. At least I'd remembered to bring one this time.

Tilting my umbrella against the wind-driven rain, I hurried for Olivia's shop, my feet and legs getting a soaking. A bell sounded as I opened the front door. Stepping inside, I quickly closed my dripping umbrella and shook it over the door mat. I was in luck. Olivia was back from the meeting and sitting behind a register, chatting amiably with two women. She glanced at the door, gave me a small wave, and then went back to her conversation.

While I waited for a private moment for our talk, I walked around the store, which was a rather odd combination of florist and stationers. Odd, but it worked in this small town, where a shop devoted to only flowers or stationery might have failed. If I bought stationery, I thought, that could soften my approach and make Olivia a little more amenable to answering a few questions. I'd be a customer then, and my nosiness more acceptable.

I wandered up and down the stationery aisles, searching for something I'd actually use, but it soon became obvious that Olivia's taste and mine didn't line up. I loved flowers, but not sprinkled all over my writing paper, and every time I picked up a box to check the price tag, I was appalled. Finally I found some inexpensive stationery that fit the bill. It was plain and light blue—a blue the manufacturer called "Robin's Egg."

I was staring at the box's label when Olivia strode up to me, greeting me as though we were long-lost friends. She was still riding high over her campaign victory. The world and everything in it was her delightful oyster.

"Rachel, it's been weeks since you were in here!" she cried.

"Olivia, congratulations," I said. "I was at the meeting."

She brushed my arm with her hand. "Thank you!"

"You're going to be very busy, aren't you? Being president, running a store."

"Oh, but it's worth it. I have so many ideas, so many things I can do for Juniper Grove. I can hardly wait."

"I heard the supermarket deal fell through."

"*That* would have been a disaster. A supermarket is the last thing we need in our town. Good riddance."

Ridiculous, I thought. But I didn't want to argue with her and risk her going silent before I could ask her about the scavenger hunt. "I'd love to get this," I said, holding up the box in my hands.

"Good choice! This way."

I trailed after her to the register and used that brief break in our conversation to come up with a smooth way to ask her about the hag clue she told the Hannafords to leave in Gina's yard. She rang up the stationery, I pulled a twenty from my jeans pocket, and she dropped the box in a white bag emblazoned with the word "Blooms." Standing there with the bag in my hand, hemming and hawing inside, I knew there was no smooth way to ask. I dove in. "Can I ask you something about the scavenger hunt?"

"Wasn't that awful?" she replied. "I'm having

nightmares about it. Are you?"

"But you didn't like Maureen."

"I'm exaggerating when I say nightmares. Maureen and I didn't get along, but I wouldn't wish murder on anyone. Our quiet little town. What happened to it?" Olivia shook her head.

"The people who run the scavenger hunt—"

"The committee."

"Yes, the committee. Are they allowed to join in?"

Olivia laughed. "That would defeat the purpose of the game since they would know where all the clues are buried."

Here goes, I thought. "But I understand you told the Hannafords that witch hats had been left out of Gina Peeler's yard and asked them to hide them there. That would give Team Main Street an advantage, wouldn't it?"

Olivia's faced clouded over. "Who told you I said that?"

The way I'd framed my question, it was rather obvious who had told me that, but I refused to say their names. "Is it true? Because Gina never agreed to sign up. The clue about the hag at Julia's checkpoint was supposed to lead people to a stuffed witch a few houses away, not Gina's yard."

Olivia watched me with unconcealed annoyance. How dare I question her. "I couldn't help it if people misinterpreted the riddles."

"That's not the point," I said, shaking my head. "Whether or not you thought the hag clue would lead to Gina's yard, you had the Hannafords leave a clue there for people to find, and Gina never signed up for the hunt."

In an instant Olivia's brows uncreased and she unpinched her lips. "There's nothing wrong with a little misdirection in a scavenger hunt. It's a strategy, Rachel."

She was changing tack, fending off my questions with a new line of defense. Nothing devious had taken place, she'd just employed a clever device to defeat the other teams. What nonsense.

"If it was a strategy, why didn't you let Jenny and Tyler Hannaford in on it? They thought Gina was part of the hunt."

"Did they? I guess I should have explained myself better." Olivia started to fussily rearrange small notepads and other office supplies scattered around the register.

"One more question," I said.

She stopped moving and looked me square in the eyes. "What now?"

"Why such an unkind clue? Why use the word 'hag'? Gina doesn't deserve that."

"How long have you lived here?"

"A little over five months."

Olivia let go with a humorless snort. "You know nothing."

"So enlighten me."

Olivia glared, and I waited.

"Fine. Gina Peeler tried to destroy me and everything I've worked for. Last week she reported me to the Health Department, telling them I was serving food to customers illegally and I had rats running around the store. Rats! I've never even seen a rat in Juniper Grove. And the food was a bowl of hard candy by the register, which is one hundred percent legal. But did that stop the Health Department from entering my store while I had customers in it? No, it did not."

"Gina would never—"

"You don't know what you're talking about, Rachel." Olivia was in full throttle, her voice turning shrill. "Gina could have ruined me. You don't own a business, so you don't understand that your store's reputation is all. If people hear you have rats and that the Health Department had to come in, that's all they need to know. They don't follow up on the rumors and find out if they're true. They go somewhere else."

I held up my hands, begging her to stop. "Wait a minute. How do you know it was Gina who called the Health Department?"

"It was clear as crystal."

"How so?"

"An acquaintance told me, and that's all I'm going to say."

"Was this acquaintance Maureen Nicholson?"

Olivia said nothing, but her stunned expression told me I'd hit the mark.

"Good grief, that woman really was a one-woman wrecking crew," I said. "Olivia, Maureen called the Health Department on Justin and told everyone that Holly's bakery failed an inspection. And those are just the two incidents I know about. She was out to make trouble for every business in Juniper Grove."

Olivia felt behind her for the register stool and sank into it. "Why would Maureen do that?"

"You said yourself she was ruthless. I think she was very unhappy too."

"Kirk. He goaded her into it."

"I wouldn't blame him. Their troubles were at least fifty-fifty, if not thirty-seventy, Maureen's fault."

"What have I done?" Olivia said, a hint of pleading in her voice.

She wasn't talking about the nasty clue, I could tell. "What *have* you done, Olivia?"

81

"I really thought it was Gina. I didn't know. I'm so sorry."

"What have you done, Olivia?"

"I'm afraid to tell you. I can't have any more trouble, especially not legal trouble. I was just elected president."

She sounded like a child, and I wasn't going to stand for it. "Whatever you've done or planned to do, can you undo it? Now?"

"I think it's too late."

"You *think* it's too late?" I planted my palms on the counter and leaned in, a foot from her startled face. "Gina doesn't deserve whatever you've done, so fix it now. Tell me what you did."

"She's all right. I told them not to hurt her or even get near her. Just her house."

I wanted to pound my fist on the counter. "What?"

"I paid some kids to break her windows early this morning, before the sun came up. I told them to make it look like a Halloween prank. You know how kids like to target old people's houses this time of year. But they're kids, Rachel, you know? Maybe they took my money and never showed up. It's possible."

CHAPTER 10

Every single window at the front of Gina's pretty yellow house was shattered. Glass littered her front porch, some of it mingling with the autumn leaves on her lawn. Even her wind chimes hadn't escaped the wrath of the vandals, who had torn them from the soffit and stomped them into the concrete.

As I stood on her brick path, wondering where I could safely put my feet, Officer Underhill appeared from around the side of the house, his trusty crime-scene camera with him. "Tell me where to walk, Officer. I don't want to step on any evidence," I said.

"Any evidence was washed away by the rain," Underhill said, mounting the porch steps.

I considered my options. I could wait for Olivia to confess, which would be best for her, or I could ease Gina's mind and help the police by speaking up right now. "I know who did this."

Underhill stopped taking photographs.

"I don't know the specific kids who did this, but I know who paid them to do it."

"Chief?" Underhill called out.

"I'll go inside," I said.

Underhill thrust out an arm. "Ma'am."

"Gina knows me," I said, sidestepping his arm and

heading inside. I liked Underhill, but sometimes he enjoyed being officious a little too much.

Gilroy was about to push open Gina's screen door when I grabbed for the handle and swung it wide.

"Rachel?" he said. "Do you two . . . ?" He threw a thumb over his shoulder, pointing to where Gina sat at her kitchen table.

"We know each other," I said.

"Please let her in," Gina said.

Gilroy stepped aside and I joined Gina at the table, giving her a hug before sitting beside her. She sagged back in her chair, worn out not just from a lack of sleep, I thought, but from the kind of exhaustion you felt when life had battered you about a little.

"How did you hear?" Gina asked.

"I know who did this." I looked from Gina to Gilroy. "Olivia Seitz paid some teenagers to break her windows. She told me herself a few minutes ago."

"Why would she do that?" Gina said. There was no anger in her voice, only sadness and confusion.

"She thought you filed a false report with the Health Department over Blooms."

"I wouldn't do that. I don't even know *how* to do that."

"Are you willing to give a statement?" Gilroy asked me.

"If you talk to Olivia, she'll admit to it. She feels bad. She knows now that it was Maureen Nicholson who filed the false report. Maureen did the same thing to Justin, and she spread rumors about Holly's store failing an inspection."

"How could she think I did that?" Gina said. "I hardly know her, and I've never even been inside her store. I've got my own flowers, and I never write anyone."

84

Gilroy was jotting in his little spiral notebook. His placid expression was no indication of what his investigation had or had not uncovered about Maureen's viciousness. For all I knew, all of this was a shocking revelation to him. Then again, he was often one step further ahead than I gave him credit for. He might have already known what Maureen did to Justin and Holly.

"When did this happen?" I asked Gina.

"About three in the morning. I was in bed. I heard the glass breaking, but I couldn't get up fast enough. By the time I got my cane and made it to the door, they were long gone. Two of my neighbors came over to check on me, so that was nice. I've got good neighbors. I waited a few hours and called the police."

"Why did you wait?"

"I didn't want to wake anyone up. What could they do? It's just glass."

"Do you have insurance?"

"Rachel, they're going to raise my rates. I won't be able to pay."

"You make her insurance company pay," Gilroy said, still jotting. "You make them pay to replace the glass and clean up your property." He slipped his pen and notebook into his suit jacket. "You and your insurance company don't pay a cent. The police report I'm going to write will help with that, but first I'll have to talk to Mrs. Seitz."

"Do I need to come to the station?" Gina asked.

"You don't need to do anything. I'm going to call a company that can board up your windows this afternoon and tell them to send the bill to Mrs. Seitz's insurance company. Then I'll find out from her the names of the kids who did this, talk to their parents, and see what help they're willing

85

to give you."

The way Gilroy said "willing" made me smile. Those parents were in for quite a visit, and by the time that visit was over, they'd be willing to do anything Gilroy asked of them.

"Do you have someplace else to stay tonight?" Gilroy asked.

"I'm not leaving," Gina said. "I'm not going to leave my home."

"You can stay with me," I offered. "I've got more than enough room, and I'd be glad to have you. I'll make tea."

"Thanks, but nope, not going to. They're not running me out of my home."

"You understand every window will be boarded up," Gilroy said. "It'll be that way for at least a couple days, and even then it might be a long process installing every window. I'll try to speed things up, but I can't promise anything."

"This house may be old, but I've got electric lights, Chief," Gina said with a grin, "and it will be much too cold to leave the windows open tonight. I'll be very cozy."

I glanced up at Gilroy. "I'll stay until the windows get boarded up."

"Good. I'll swing by with a copy of the report when I've written it, Mrs. Peeler, and I'll give you a call about the windows. I'm sorry about this, but we'll get it fixed, and you'll end up getting new windows out of it."

After Gilroy and Underhill left, Gina and I made tea and took cups out to her porch. I grabbed a broom from her kitchen and cleared broken glass from the chairs, table, and the porch around our feet. We sat in silence for a while, sipping cinnamon tea, enjoying the light breeze in the aftermath of the storm, and taking in, as best we could, the destruction around us.

Gina broke the silence. "They smashed my wind chimes. Have you noticed that some people want to destroy beautiful things?"

"I have. But the stupid kids who did this were paid to cause destruction. They weren't thinking of beauty, ugliness, or anything else. Just money."

"What made Olivia think I'd call the Health Department on her store?"

"That's easy. Maureen told her you did."

Gina gaped. "The very same Maureen who called the department on Justin Miller and spread rumors about Holly's bakery? Olivia should have known better than to believe her."

"For some reason she was predisposed to think it was you."

"Yeah." Gina absentmindedly played with one of her numerous gray dreadlocks, kneading a turquoise bead between her thumb and forefinger. "You're probably right."

At first I thought it best not to tell Gina anything else I'd found out about Olivia, but I quickly reconsidered. She deserved to know the full truth. "Olivia was also the one who had Jenny and Tyler Hannaford put the witch hats in your yard and plant the hag clue at the first checkpoint. The Hannafords thought you'd signed up for the hunt. They didn't know you weren't part of it."

"Olivia doesn't even know me."

"That's just it, Gina. It's not personal, as silly as that sounds. She didn't care who you were. She thought you were trying to ruin her business and went a little nuts. If it helps any, she feels terrible."

"As well she should." Gina gave me a sly grin. "But

87

life is too short to hold grudges. It's a beautiful fall day, and I'm getting new windows."

"Brand spanking new."

"Two of my old windows had cracks in them."

"The new ones won't."

Gina raised her teacup in a toast to her new windows. In the midst of broken glass and shattered wind chimes, she had found a great big silver lining. It was remarkable.

"How's your investigation coming?" she asked.

"Slowly. It's been eye-opening learning about Maureen. She must have been a miserable woman, lashing out at so many people for no reason."

"If you ask me, Olivia has some issues herself. Maureen was in competition with her, not me. It makes you wonder what crazy thing she would have done if she'd known Maureen was the Health Department informant." Gina pulled in her breath sharply. "What if . . . ?"

She didn't need to finish her sentence. "If Olivia knew it was Maureen who called the department, she wouldn't have gone after you."

"That doesn't mean she didn't kill Maureen."

"They all claim to be friends and business associates—Jenny, Tyler, Olivia, Justin—but I sense jealousy and suspicion when they're together. They don't like each other very much. Even when they're smiling and shaking hands. It's possible even Jenny and Tyler don't like each other." I told Gina about the election results, how Olivia had won the presidency of the Juniper Grove Development Association and Jenny congratulated her. She didn't seem surprised.

"Olivia is higher up in the pecking order of the Juniper Grove intelligentsia," she said.

"Was Olivia ever at a Juniper Grove Vegetarian

Society meeting?"

"Oh, no. Olivia likes a good cut of meat. Beef and pork."

"How about Justin?"

"The steakhouse owner?" she chuckled.

"He recently added vegetarian dishes to his menu. I saw Jenny Hannaford eating there, and she and Justin seem to be very close."

"I never saw him at a vegetarian meeting, but he might have started attending after I quit."

"Jenny didn't quit after Maureen fed her beef?"

"No need to. Maureen was politely asked not to return." Gina laughed softly and tilted back her head, taking in the sun's pale rays.

Everything I'd heard about Maureen painted an ugly picture of an ambitious woman who set no limits on her behavior, but I wondered if there was another side to her I wasn't hearing. The only person who could tell me was Kirk Nicholson. He'd told me my investigation into his wife's murder had his blessing. It was time to find out if he truly meant that.

Chief Gilroy was true to his word. Two hours later, as an early evening chill set in, a window company from Fort Collins rolled up to Gina's house and began to board her windows. The crew told her if all went well, they could begin to install her windows Friday morning, only two days away. Minutes after that, a cleanup crew arrived and began to rake glass from her lawn.

Gina offered them cinnamon tea, but they all declined, which was for the best, considering its powerful sinus-clearing properties. She gave me Kirk's approximate address—somewhere on Forest Street—and I helped her inside to her living room.

"You're going alone to see Kirk?" she asked, dropping into a two-seater couch and propping her cane against the other cushion. "Uninvited?"

I told her yes, I was heading over there right now, though there was no guarantee I'd find his house.

"I'm sure it's white, and I know there isn't a pumpkin patch in the front yard," she said. "But be careful what you say to him. He had as much reason to murder Maureen as anyone else, and if he did, he's not going to appreciate your questions."

When I left Gina, she was in front of her television, happy as could be. Happier, in fact, than if the window breaking had never happened. As soon as I got the chance, I'd tell Gilroy that. He'd been as troubled as Gina about the damage to her house. He hated cruelty, I knew that much about him. But cruelty toward the defenseless? Not on his watch. Not in his town.

CHAPTER 11

What distinguished Kirk's house from the other white houses without pumpkin patches on Forest Street was that his was the only one displaying three carved pumpkins on the porch, the middle one with a big blue ribbon hanging from its stem. Maureen's prize-winning carving. Before I knocked on Kirk's door, I bent low to study it, and I had to agree with Julia—whoever had carved it possessed lots of time and talent. I knocked on the Nicholsons' red door and waited, sure I'd be turned away the moment Kirk opened it. To my surprise, he welcomed me inside, almost as though he'd been expecting me.

His living room was sparsely furnished in a palette of soft, neutral colors, giving it a clean, modern look. Not something I would have associated with Kirk, but then, the decor had probably been Maureen's doing. He directed me to one of a pair of armchairs astride a fireplace and then sat opposite me. Instantly, he rose. "I forgot my manners. Do you want something to drink?"

"No, thank you. I don't need anything."

He sat again. "You're here to ask me about Maureen."

"And other people," I replied. "If you don't mind."

"You've talked to everyone else, so why not?"

"I think your perspective must be very different."

"In some ways, yes. In other ways I see her just like

everyone else does."

I pointed back toward the door. "I saw her prize-winning pumpkin on your porch. It's amazing."

A slow smile spread across Kirk's face. "Have you heard about the fury it caused? Maureen wins the blue ribbon and their world falls apart."

"Their?"

"That whole bunch. Justin, Olivia, Eric, Jenny. Oh, no"—he wiggled his hands in the air—"someone besides the great Justin Miller won the contest this year."

"Justin did seem especially upset," I said.

Kirk guffawed and gave his considerable nose a scratch, working a forefinger under his nostrils. "I know he takes the contest seriously, but I can't. Can you? It's pumpkin carving. It's meant to be fun. Or it *was* meant to be fun."

"I heard Maureen hired someone to carve it, and I think that's what they were upset about."

Kirk's smile grew. "She didn't hire anyone. I carved it."

It had never crossed my mind that he'd carved the pumpkin. But of course.

"I didn't see the big deal," Kirk went on. "I used to whittle a lot, so I'm good with the small carving and paring knives you need for the detail. Besides, I enjoy it. I carved that winner on the porch in front of the TV one night. It was simple."

"No one else knows this?"

"Not until yesterday. That's when I decided to tell Justin. We were arguing about it when you saw us outside the Porter Grill."

I flopped back in my seat. "That's what that argument

92

was about?"

"Nothing more than that. Just a pumpkin. See why I can't take it or them seriously? Anyway, when Maureen won, she was happy for once. I was willing to carve a pumpkin just to see her smile for the first time in months."

"She was happy you carved the pumpkin or happy she won the contest?" My question was blunter than I'd intended, and as soon as the words left my mouth, I braced myself for an angry reply. Instead of anger, I received a compliment.

"A very astute question, Rachel. The answer is the contest. She beat Justin, and in that way she beat them all. You know they were in high school together, don't you?" He crossed the living room, opened a cabinet at the base of a bookcase, and removed a large book, holding it aloft for me to see. "The Juniper Grove High yearbook."

"No, I didn't know."

Kirk brought the yearbook back to his chair and started flipping through the back pages. "They weren't all in the same grade, but for one year, they were all at the Juniper Grove High together. Justin and Olivia were seniors, Maureen and Tyler were sophomores, and Jenny was a freshman. I'd already graduated by then."

"Were they friends?"

"More than friends and less than friends," Kirk said, handing me the open yearbook and tapping a photo of his wife. "That's Maureen in her sophomore year."

Such a young, innocent face, I thought. *With no trace of the ambition and unkindness to come.*

"Maureen and Jenny didn't get along, even then, but Jenny was a freshman—you know how that is. She was the kid who kept hanging around, the one everyone had to tolerate. Tyler got along with everybody, but he wasn't really close to any of them, I think. Justin and Olivia were the big kids that everyone looked up to. Turn back to the letter-M names. Miller."

I flipped the pages until I found Justin Miller's senior photo. "He had hair back then."

"All the girls were crazy about him. I mean all of them."

I looked up.

"That's right. Olivia, Maureen, and Jenny. They all wanted him. But only Olivia was graduating in the same class as he was. She and Justin were going to be adults, while Maureen and Jenny were going to be left behind in high school." Kirk leaned back, and I could tell by the expression on his face he was about to deliver the kicker. "Guess who Justin took to the senior prom? Maureen."

"Really? I would have guessed Olivia."

"Sure. They were both seniors, so it makes sense. At first Maureen was sure Justin would ask Olivia or even Jenny—she told me that after we married. I don't know all that went on before he finally asked Maureen, but I do know there were a lot of hurt feelings. That's when Maureen became a bully. Not her words—mine. She saw what she wanted, and she found out she could get it by pushing people around and telling lies behind their backs. It worked. She got Justin at the prom."

It brought to mind what Justin had said in the Porter Grill about Maureen always being a kid at school, always bullying. You could only appease her temporarily, not stop her, he'd said. So Maureen had learned the tricks of the bullying trade in high school, in her quest to win Justin. "Why are you telling me this, Kirk?"

"Justin asking Maureen to the prom started more than two decades of backstabbing and competition, and it ended with this election to the Juniper Grove Development Association. It's no accident that Jenny, Olivia, and my wife were all running for president. I'm only surprised Justin didn't throw his hat into the ring. I meant to ask him why he didn't, but instead I told him I'd carved the pumpkin. Not sure why."

I knew why. He had wanted to pay Justin back for his wife wanting him more than twenty years ago. Why didn't they all stay away from one another? Even in a small town there were ways to avoid people who rubbed you the wrong way. They all seemed to feed off one another. Liking and hating each other like high school kids, never really able to graduate and get past those days. "Did you hear that Olivia won the vote?"

"Yeah, I heard. I was going to go and stand up for Maureen. One of her high school buddies killed her because she was going to win again and they couldn't bear it. If she were alive, she'd be president of the association now."

"Kirk, you yourself said Maureen bullied people." *And suffered the natural consequences of her actions*, I almost added.

"She did. I'm not going to lie. Heck, she bullied me. We were getting a divorce, and she wanted everything I owned. The house, the car. Not that she was going to get it, but she was going to try to make my life as unpleasant as she could in the meantime. A part of me still loves her, but I didn't want to live with her anymore. I signed the final divorce papers the day she died. She never got a chance to sign them."

"You said she wanted the house. Would she have

gotten it after the divorce was final? Is it yours now?"

"Those are police kinds of questions."

"You told me to investigate, with your blessing."

Kirk sat forward and looked intently at me. "Maureen was going to get the house, and I was going to get the car and our bank account. It was a price I was eager to pay. It meant my freedom and happy days again. I wouldn't jeopardize that freedom by committing murder. Anyway, I've told you, I didn't hate her."

"The house is yours?"

"The house is mine."

Thunder sounded, signaling the arrival of another storm, and at that instant it struck me forcefully that I might be sitting in the house of a killer—at night, without any defense. And only Gina knew where I'd gone.

"The others weren't blameless," Kirk continued, oblivious to my discomfort. "Don't you see that now? You've talked to them. You see them for what they are."

I inched forward until I was sitting on the edge of my chair, a position from which I could stand and run, or fight, if I had to. "What I see is a group of people who fight over pumpkins and old proms, and a woman who hated her old classmates so much she tried to ruin them."

"Then you're seeing things right and you stand a chance of solving Maureen's murder."

"You still think it has to do with the supermarket and the association."

"There was no greater controversy in this town, and all of them were part of it. But I think they've wanted to kill each other for years."

Perplexed by his choice of words, I asked him what he meant. "Jenny and Olivia were friendly after the election," I told him. "So were Tyler and Justin."

"Don't let that fool you. They're all still in high school."

Maybe Kirk was in such pain he couldn't see that his wife had caused a lot of misery in recent weeks. I didn't buy that one of her old high school friends had murdered her over either a long-ago prom or a supermarket.

I rose, made an apology for my swift exit, and strode for the door. I couldn't sit in his armchair any longer, wondering if he might reveal himself as the killer. I still didn't think he was, but I was now taking unnecessary chances. I vowed silently that my next meeting with a suspect would be in public.

"If you have any more questions, give me a call," Kirk said, following me. "I'm in the online white pages."

I felt safer once I was on his porch and he was just inside the door, hands thrust in his pockets. Again I admired his pumpkin-carving expertise, and again he congratulated himself on his stealth.

"Kirk, did Maureen say anything about meeting someone the night of the scavenger hunt?"

"Not that I know of. Why?"

"I think someone lured her with the promise of information on a flash drive."

"That drive they found in your friend's backpack?"

"So she didn't tell you she was going to meet with someone Monday night?"

"No, but we weren't speaking much. She told everyone I was out of town."

I started for his porch steps but circled back. "Here's something I don't understand. If all this began back in high school, why did it flare up now?"

"I told you, the Juniper Grove Development Association and the supermarket."

"What about the false Health Department reports?"

"Nothing new there. She lied all the time. The false reports were just another lie. And they got back at her by telling everyone her pastries at Coffee and Cakes were like cardboard."

"What about Jenny and Tyler's businesses? They're both managers."

"I'm sure she started rumors about them too. And vice versa."

I thanked Kirk and trotted down the steps for my car, still not convinced that he was a killer, but relieved nonetheless to be out of his house. His interpretation of events didn't sit right with me. These people had been at each other's throats for years without one of them killing the other, and then, boom, Maureen runs for president of the JGDA and one of them murders her for it? I didn't buy that the campaign had boiled over into murder any more than I bought that high school memories had. No, I was missing a vital piece of information, and I had no idea where to look for it.

CHAPTER 12

"I can't believe you went to Kirk Nicholson's house alone," Julia said. "What if something had happened to you?"

"Gina knew where I was."

"How would Gina know if you made it home? You could still be there this morning, trapped in his house, and I'd have no idea." She glared at me over the rim of her coffee cup, took a long, noisy sip, and set the cup down hard. "Don't ever do that again. Friends are hard to come by."

I couldn't help but smile. "I promise."

"Though you did learn a few things."

"That I did. Let's take our coffee out to my porch. It's a sunny morning."

We settled into my metal porch chairs, both recent purchases from a garage sale, and enjoyed the warmth of the sun as it shone in slivers through the pine trees across the street. Soon my front yard would be bathed in sunlight. My rose garden was no more, the victim of a hard freeze earlier in the month, but all around me, up and down Finch Hill Road, were the colors of autumn—red hedges, orange maples, yellow cottonwoods—and the cool, crisp air was lifting my spirits.

"Did you talk to Holly yesterday?" I asked Julia.

"Last night, when you were out endangering yourself."

"How's she doing?"

"Better. The boy who wrote 'Murderer' on the bakery window cleaned it up yesterday, and his parents told him he was going to work for her for the next four Saturdays without pay. Holly said Chief Gilroy suggested that. He could have arrested the little monster."

"He's about Caleb's age, Julia. Kids that age make foolish choices. This is better."

"I suppose."

I breathed in the clean, cool air, feeling my muscles relax and my mind clear itself of a jumble of facts, many of them unrelated and useless to my investigation. Instincts alone were telling me that the answer to Maureen's murder lay in an as-yet-undiscovered fact, but I trusted my instincts. "I'm sitting here trying to picture Justin Miller as Juniper Grove High's heartthrob, and I can't quite make the leap."

"Neither can I," Julia said with a laugh. "Not that there's anything wrong with him, but *three* women?"

"I wonder how that made Tyler feel."

"Like a fifth wheel. Do you think he could have killed Maureen?"

"A fifth wheel would want to eliminate the competition."

"You mean Justin," Julia said.

"And that's only if Justin's status as a man who won the hearts of all three high school friends was the cause of Maureen's murder."

"You don't think it was."

"I'm almost positive it wasn't."

I downed the rest of my coffee, and for a while I sat without speaking, juggling suspects and motives in my mind. One thing became clear to me: I needed to start fresh. The old Juniper Grove High friends, if they could be called that, had managed to live many years beyond their high school days without killing one another. Although the teenage trauma of those days had engendered hurt feelings that had never fully healed, the trigger for murder had to be in the very recent past.

"What are your plans for today?" Julia asked.

"I need to talk to Justin and find out who his friend in the Health Department is. The one who told him Maureen filed a report on his restaurant."

"Maybe Holly knows."

"I don't want to bother Holly about it. Besides, she never told us about the false rumors Maureen spread. She didn't want us to know." I cringed, suddenly remembering I'd told Olivia what Maureen had done to Holly. "Though I did mention it to Olivia when I was explaining to her that it was Maureen, not Gina, who reported *her* store to the Health Department."

"What a tangled web!"

"I also need to talk to Peter."

"Holly's Peter?"

I stood and gathered our coffee cups. "I think he was a junior at Juniper Grove High when Justin and the others were there. He might be able to tell me something."

"Holly said he'd be at the bakery this morning. Let me grab my purse."

"You're going?"

"Who's going to keep you out of trouble?" she shouted as she scurried back to her house.

Ten minutes later we were parked outside Holly's Sweets on Main Street. All of downtown Juniper Grove, an area of only four blocks east to west and three blocks north to south, was about a four-minute drive from my house.

101

When I'd lived in Boston, I'd avoided downtown, but Juniper Grove's little downtown was different. It was a neighborhood more than a business district, and after only five months in town, the face of almost every shop owner there was familiar to me, as mine was to them.

Holly grinned broadly as we entered her bakery, which I took as a good sign, seeing as she wasn't hiding from customers like she had the last time we'd walked through her door. Not wanting to sidetrack my investigation, I averted my eyes from some lovely powdered-sugar cream puffs she had deviously placed front and center in the display case.

"Your shop window is sparkling clean," I said.

"Did Julia tell you?"

I nodded. "I don't think that boy will bother you anymore."

"He's basically a good kid."

Julia grumbled in disagreement.

"Good or bad, he's ours for the next four Saturdays," Holly said. "If this vandalism keeps up, I'll never have to hire another part-timer."

When the bakery had been the victim of vandalism in September, in a far more serious attack, the vandal had been sentenced to help Holly and Peter for three months, courtesy of Chief Gilroy. That boy was still working out his sentence with a mop and broom.

I told Holly about Gina's broken windows so she wouldn't feel she was the only one in town to suffer as a result of mistaken identity, and then I moved on to the subject of Peter and his school days. "Was Peter in high school the same time Justin Miller was?"

"Sure he was," Holly answered. "Maureen too. He talked about her the night she was killed. Justin was gone by

102

the time I started high school. I remember Jenny Hannaford, but only vaguely."

"You and Justin became friends later?"

"After I opened the bakery. He was so kind to me and Peter, offering us help and suggestions."

"Can I ask Peter a few questions? He might be able to shed some light on them."

Three women, their eyes focused like lasers on the display case, entered the store, eagerly chattering about their favorite pastries. Holly waved us to the back of the bakery, called out for Peter, and then headed back to the register.

"Julia, Rachel," Peter said, wiping his flour-covered hands on a towel. "I haven't seen you two in a while. What can I do you for?"

"A scone would be nice," Julia said.

"Coming up."

"You're shameless," I whispered as Peter grabbed a fresh scone from a baking sheet.

"Raspberry?"

"Lovely."

"Rachel?"

"I'm buying cream puffs on the way out," I said.

Julia huffed and bit into her scone.

"Okay, so . . ." Looking weary already at nine o'clock in the morning, Peter dropped onto a stool, brushing a sliver of flour or powdered sugar from his chin. Though Irish by name, I'd always thought he had the broad face and slightly upturned nose of someone with Scandinavian heritage. A pleasant face, I thought. And a good man. Holly had done well.

"We won't keep you long. Can you tell me anything about Maureen Nicholson, Justin Miller, and their friends at

103

Juniper Grove High? What were they like? How did they act around each other?"

"Interesting question. Holly and I were talking about that. They were friends—in a way. They also fought a lot. Justin was the leader and the others were followers. I think that's because except for Olivia, they were all younger. When I was at school I used to wonder why Justin hung around them. I was a junior at the time, but even so, seniors didn't want to hang around me. When you're eighteen, you think of younger students as kids, but Justin seemed to like them."

"I've heard that Maureen, Olivia, and Jenny had a thing for Justin."

Peter chuckled and smiled at the memory. "That's true. But it was Maureen and Justin who went to the senior prom together. They were in the running for prom king and queen, but another couple won. Can't remember who they were."

"I wonder why Justin didn't ask Olivia since they were both seniors."

"He should have. I heard later that he and Maureen argued all night. I don't know what they argued about, though. You know how it was back then. Senior proms were private, and when seniors left school, the younger students rarely saw them again. That summer Maureen wasn't around much—or at least I didn't see her—but I saw the rest of them together downtown."

"Tyler Hannaford too?"

"Yep. I think that's about the time he and Jenny started dating—when she turned sixteen. They dated all next year at school."

Julia took a break from her scone to echo the word "sixteen" and remind us that Jenny had been only fifteen

104

when she first began to go out with Justin and the others.

"Did they all stay in touch after Justin graduated?" I asked.

"I don't know how close they were after high school, but every once in a while I'd see them together, usually without Maureen."

"But sometimes with her?"

"Rarely, but yes, sometimes."

"Do you think Maureen was in love with Justin?"

Peter tilted his head back slightly, contemplating the question. "Probably. More than Olivia and Jenny were, anyway. They had high school crushes on him, the big senior, but they got over him quickly. Jenny dated Tyler and Olivia found Eric. Both couples seem happy to me, though you can never tell."

"Did Justin ever marry?"

"No, but he was a workaholic. About a year out of high school there didn't seem to be much room for anything in his life but work. He opened the Porter Grill when he was in his early thirties, and the restaurant business is a demanding one."

"One more thing," I said. "Maureen was divorcing her husband. Do you think she wanted to get back together with Justin after all these years?"

Peter chuckled. "Wouldn't that be weird? I don't know, but one thing I've learned is that some people never really leave high school."

"Well, we've kept you long enough."

"No problem. It gave me a chance to sit for the first time this morning," Peter said, pushing to his feet again.

"The bakery business is demanding too," I said. "We're glad the kid who wrote on your window was caught.

How's Caleb doing?"

"Caleb is going to be helping out here for the next two Saturdays, without pay."

"Oh, the poor boy," Julia said. "He was defending his mother's reputation."

"He should have called the police, Julia, not punched the kid in the face," Peter said.

Though Peter no doubt meant what he said, I sensed a touch of pride in his voice. Caleb had defended his mother from an outrageous charge, and a not-too-small part of Peter wanted to brag about it.

On the way out, I bought two cream puffs. And ignored Julia's rolling eyes while charitably not mentioning that I'd just watched her devour a raspberry scone. I had planned to start walking again on the trail behind my house, now that the weather was reliably cool, but so far my plans hadn't advanced to the actual doing phase.

"There's Tyler and Olivia," Julia said, discreetly pointing across the street. "They're not happy."

The two were arguing—Olivia leaning in, Tyler responding by pulling back and raking his fingers through his bangs, Olivia taking half a step back and then leaning in further. Without words and from a short distance, it resembled a dance. "They stop talking every time someone walks by," I said.

"If they want privacy, they should get off the sidewalk. What have they got to argue about? They're young, they have jobs."

"I was just thinking, Julia. Tyler's been the odd man out through all of this. He still is—just like he was in high school. Look at them arguing. Olivia's the one in control."

Watching them, I knew I'd only scratched the surface

of what made Tyler, Olivia, and the rest of the old high school gang tick. Each of them had revealed only what they had wanted me to know. It was time to dig deeper.

CHAPTER 13

In my fascination with Olivia and Tyler's argument, I hadn't noticed Jenny standing half a block up the street, also watching them. She stood in the middle of the sidewalk, oblivious to people trying to work their way around her.

Now was the time to dig deeper. "Follow me," I said to Julia, taking off in Jenny's direction and trying not to jostle the Holly's Sweets box in my hands. As I neared Jenny, I slowed my pace, hoping our meeting would seem coincidental.

I greeted her, telling her I'd seen her speech at the JGDA meeting, but it was only when I said she might have given Maureen a run for her money that she tore her eyes from the scene across the street.

"I don't think so," she said, pulling her purse strap back up on her shoulder. "Maureen had it wrapped up. Like she had everything wrapped up."

"Do you think it was because of her support for the supermarket?"

"No." Her eyes slipped across the street once more.

"Were both you and Olivia against it?"

"Yes, but I could have gone either way."

"Jenny."

She finally looked at me.

"You know I'm investigating Maureen's death."

"Are you still playing private investigator, Rachel?"

"I'm trying to help Holly."

"I know, you told me."

"What made Maureen go sour on all her friends?"

Jenny folded her arms over her chest, taking a defiant stance. "Friends? That's not the word I would use."

"You were all friends once, back in high school."

Her eyebrows arched in surprise, she said, "Who told you that?"

"It's true, isn't it?" I asked, studiously avoiding her question.

Trying for cool detachment, and failing at it, Jenny laughed lightheartedly. "A long, long time ago. Are you still close to *your* high school friends?"

"So why did Maureen turn on all of you? She fed you beef stew that she claimed was vegetarian and made false reports to the Health Department about Justin's restaurant and Olivia's store. That's pretty vicious."

Jenny eyed me suspiciously.

"Justin and Olivia told me all about it," I said. But I was dancing around my real questions, and Jenny was about to lose patience with me. "Do you know why Maureen asked to join your group at the scavenger hunt?"

"You're full of questions today," Jenny said.

Julia mumbled something unintelligible and proceeded to rake Jenny over the coals—or what passed for coals with Julia. "Now you listen, Jenny Hannaford. We're trying to help our friend Holly. Her son is being bullied at school and she's being called a murderer. Sweet Holly, who wouldn't hurt anyone. You have no reason not to answer Rachel's questions, especially since everyone knows you couldn't stand Maureen anyway. Now stop being an obstructionist and speak up."

Gaping at Julia, Jenny dropped her hands, rattling the bangles on her wrist. "I'm sorry. I just feel . . . uncomfortable."

She shot another look across the street, and this time I followed her line of sight. Olivia and Tyler had moved on.

"Would you like to talk somewhere else?" I asked. "My car's over there."

"Not that kind of uncomfortable. I don't like talking about Maureen."

"Speaking ill of the dead," Julia said with a commiserating nod.

Jenny appeared slightly amused by Julia's old-fashioned sense of propriety. "No. As a matter of fact, I speak ill of her anytime I talk about her. I just don't want to talk about her." She turned her gaze to me. "Have you ever left something behind in the past?"

Immediately I thought of Brent, the man who had asked me for my hand in marriage. And I lied. "Sure."

"Do you want to dig it up again or move on?" Jenny didn't give me time to answer. "I know how awful this sounds, but with Maureen dead, I can move on and not keep looking over my shoulder. I don't have to wonder what stupid thing she's going to do next to me or my friends, or what club I'm in that she's going to join just to get on my nerves, or what office she's going to run for just to bug me."

With the three of us clogging up the sidewalk and Jenny not wanting to go to my car, I edged toward the curb, motioning for Jenny and Julia to follow suit. When Jenny instead made a move to leave, I quickly asked another question. "I thought you'd all been friendly, or at least polite, until recently. How long has Maureen been harassing you?"

110

Despite her protestations, Jenny very much wanted to talk about Maureen. She promptly joined Julia and me at the curb. "She comes and goes, like a volcano. She's peaceful for a few years, then she erupts. But she's been a pain in the neck since high school. Thinking back, I'm not sure she ever liked any of us. You don't do to friends what she's done to us."

"But she asked to join Team Main Street for the scavenger hunt."

"You don't understand Maureen. She did that to annoy us. She knew we wouldn't, or couldn't, say no. Same with my vegetarian club. Maureen wasn't a vegetarian and she wasn't interested in becoming one." As Jenny talked, her gaze kept straying to the other side of the street, searching.

"So she knew how all of you felt about her?"

"It didn't make any difference." She twisted back, checking the sidewalk behind her.

"But Maureen did like one of you. Justin."

Jenny's eyes shot back to mine.

"In fact, she loved him," I went on. "But so did you and Olivia."

For a moment, Jenny seemed to have lost the power of speech.

"Did this anger between you all start because of a high school prom?" I asked.

Casting her eyes upward, Jenny let loose with an exaggerated sigh. "You're talking about the prom now? The *prom*?"

"Justin chose Maureen."

"We were kids."

"But Maureen still loved Justin."

It was a wild leap, suggesting that Maureen was still in

love with her old prom date, but I needed to see Jenny's reaction. To my surprise, she nodded, her expression one of grim affirmation.

"I think she loved him more now than she did back then." Her shoulders rose in a shrug. "Maybe it's because she was getting older and she remembered how life used to be. Plus, Justin never married, so maybe she saw her chance."

"But Justin wasn't interested."

"No, not at all."

"And then Maureen cheated in the pumpkin-carving contest, which must have made him angry."

"Justin didn't care about the stupid pumpkin." Jenny hitched her fallen purse strap back on her shoulder. "It was about the cheating. I have to go. To tell you the truth, I really don't care who killed Maureen, and I'm not sure I want to help you find out."

"But Holly—" Julia began.

"Holly didn't kill her. Everyone knows that, so stop worrying." Jenny wheeled away from us and disappeared up the sidewalk at warp speed.

"She's hiding something," Julia said.

"They're all hiding something."

Julia made a small clucking sound, like a slightly irritated hen. "Can we get into your car now? My feet aren't what they used to be."

Back in the Forester, I reached around and gently set my cream puff box on the back seat. "I wonder which has more calories, a cream puff or a scone."

"That's your breakfast tomorrow, is it?" Julia said, curling her lip.

I stared through the windshield at the foothills and the

high peaks beyond them, which were speckled in snow like one of Holly's powdered-sugar pastries. "Kirk Nicholson told me they're all still in high school. I think he was right. The more they protest that they've moved on, the more I think they're stuck in the past."

"There's Chief Gilroy coming out of Town Hall," Julia said with a sudden lilt in her voice. "Doesn't he look nice? But then he always looks nice."

"He wears cowboy boots."

"But not fancy ones. Sensible ones. Man ones."

"I didn't notice until yesterday."

"There's trouble," Julia said, indicating with a jerk of her head that I should look farther up the sidewalk.

Jenny Hannaford had done an about-face and was now heading back down the sidewalk, waving and shouting, heading straight for Gilroy. He halted midstep and turned to her.

"Look at her arms flipping around," I said. "She's furious."

Julia, clearly in a sarcastic mood, said, "I can't imagine why. Everyone likes to be grilled on their past by a stranger."

"Do you think she's talking about me?"

"You can bet your cream puffs on it."

I leaned back on my car's headrest. "I need to find the killer before Gilroy stops me."

"He's trying to find the killer too."

"I know he is, but I think he's looking in the wrong places. Like that flash drive. He'll never find fingerprints or anything else on that drive. It was just a means to draw Maureen, like the clue the killer handed her during the hunt. They were meant to draw her to the Andersons' yard on the night of their anniversary, when they'd be out celebrating.

113

Did you know it was their anniversary?"

"Everyone who's lived here for a while knew. Everyone knows everyone."

"Gilroy's probably focusing on the knife too—where it came from, were there fingerprints on it—but he won't find anything."

"But he has to look. It's his job."

"He's looking at the paper the clue was printed on, and the printer that was used, but Maureen's killer isn't stupid. That clue was probably printed out a week or more ago, maybe in Fort Collins or Denver."

Whatever Gilroy was saying to Jenny, it was working. Her hands now hung limply at her sides, and her face, creased in anger just moments ago, had relaxed. She nodded. She flicked back her thick blonde hair and smiled coyly. She grabbed a strand of it and twirled it between her fingers.

"Gilroy knows how to play it, doesn't he?" I said.

"Play what?"

"Just look at her twirling her hair, giggling."

"Jenny?"

"Never mind." I started the engine.

"I thought you were going to ask Justin about his friend in the Health Department."

"Later. It's not that important."

"So where are we going?"

"Anyplace but downtown." I checked my rearview mirror, yanked on my steering wheel, and started from the curb.

"Gilroy's waving at you to stop."

I stomped on my brake. "Why?"

"How do I know?"

Gilroy rambled over to my window and made a circular

motion with his finger. I forced a smile and rolled down the window.

"I just had a complaint from Mrs. Hannaford," he said.

"Oh, really?"

He bent low and propped his forearm on the window frame. "Rachel, you can't question people who don't want to be questioned."

"It's not like I forced her to speak to me. She had no objections when I was talking to her."

"That's true, Chief," Julia said in my defense.

"She has an objection now," Gilroy said.

"All of a sudden, when she's talking to you?" Pretending bewilderment, I made an exaggerated face. "Gosh, why would that be?"

"I don't know," Gilroy said evenly. He either hadn't caught or was choosing to ignore my snide remark. "But Mrs. Hannaford isn't the first to complain."

"Let me guess. Olivia Seitz? Justin Miller?"

Gilroy straightened. "Rachel, I'm serious."

"You're never anything but."

"There are things called restraining orders."

"So get one. Either that or arrest me. Better yet, do your job and find the killer so half the town doesn't blame Holly and torture Caleb at school."

An expression of utter bewilderment came over Gilroy's face. I could hear Julia beside me, sputtering under her breath, probably wanting to elbow me into silence.

"Is it all right if I go now, Chief?" I asked. "May I?"

"Sure," he said, stepping back from my car. He left without another word and walked off in the direction of the police station.

Julia and I were silent as we drove back to Finch Hill

115

Road, the tension in the car palpable. Sure I'd acted like a lunatic, again, but Gilroy was nothing but a con man, using his smooth mannerisms, good looks, and cowboy boots to charm the gullible women of Juniper Grove. And I'd foolishly thought he might be interested in me. I chuckled and Julia began to fume.

"What was that about?" she said. "You hurt his feelings."

"Only because he threatened me with a restraining order," I said, lying through my teeth. "Can you believe the nerve of him?"

CHAPTER 14

I said no to Julia's invitation to watch television at her house that night. My plan was to solve Maureen's murder—if I had to stay up all night—and show James Gilroy that although I couldn't giggle and flip my thick blonde hair, I could crack a murder case. While he ate donuts or whatever he'd been doing with his time since the murder.

I sat on the edge of my office desk and studied the corkboard. Was the answer in front of me, or was the crucial piece of the puzzle still missing, as I had come to believe? I'd barely had time to ask myself the question when my doorbell rang. I opened the door and Holly breezed in, bursting with excitement. Something Holly rarely did at seven o'clock at night.

"I saw your office light on," she said. "I have something you're going to want to hear."

"If it's about the case," I said. "I need to keep my focus," I added, watching Holly head for the stairs. Apparently it *was* about the case.

Holly was at the corkboard, pointing at Maureen's name, when I entered the office. "This woman was up to something bad," she declared, "and I heard it straight from the horse's mouth. Or the horse's husband's mouth."

"Kirk?"

"He was cleaning out her clothes and found a small

journal taped to the underside of a chest drawer. He was in the bakery today buying some pastry and asked me to tell you."

"Wow. I wondered about a journal. It makes sense she'd keep a record of her schemes. What did she write?"

"She wasn't specific—for the most part."

"That would be too easy." I settled into my office chair, but Holly, too agitated to sit, paced the room.

"Kirk said you asked him if she was meeting anyone the night of the scavenger hunt, and at the time he didn't know. But it turns out she wrote that she was meeting an old friend that night."

I sat to attention.

"Unfortunately, she didn't say who, but this friend was going to give her information on another one of her old friends. Kirk said she put 'friends' in quote marks."

"Information on the flash drive."

"She said they would all finally get what they deserved."

"No kidding."

"Even Justin. That's where she got more specific."

I leaned forward, stunned by what I was hearing. "Justin would get what he deserved? What exactly did she write?"

"That he never loved her, though she'd never stopped loving him, that his true love was his restaurant, and that the friend she was meeting had promised her information that would destroy the Porter Grill."

Holly stopped her pacing and stood triumphantly in front of me, hands spread wide. "Big clue?"

"Big clue," I said with a grin.

The doorbell rang again. "I may as well be in Boston,"

I said.

"I bet that's Julia. You know she watches the street like a sentry. I'll get the door."

In all my months in Juniper Grove, the only time I'd ever seen Holly move with such energy was at the bakery or on a Sunday, her day off. Six days a week she rose at four in the morning to head for Holly's Sweets, and six days a week she drew in her wings like a tired bird by seven o'clock. I knew she loved her life at the bakery, but I worried about her sometimes. She worked too hard. I didn't want her to end up tired and haggard looking—like Justin Miller.

"I'm explaining it, Julia," Holly said, jogging back to my office.

Julia, somewhat breathless behind her, managed to ask if Maureen had given the name of the old friend she was meeting.

"All she wrote was 'an old friend,'" Holly said. "It has to be one of her high school buddies. We've always thought it was, but this is proof." Holly spun on her heels and zeroed in on me. "You need to tell Chief Gilroy about this tomorrow."

"Kirk didn't report it?"

"Only to me. He doesn't like talking to the police these days."

"You tell Gilroy, Holly. It's your discovery."

"I could, but I thought you'd want a chance to talk to him. He'll be thrilled you found it out, and even if he isn't, it'll give you an excuse to talk."

"The only time Gilroy is thrilled is when he's chewing me out, and I refuse to give him another opportunity."

Julia threw her head back, giving me a not-again expression. "Heaven help us."

"You know I'm right, Julia." I seized a pen from my desk, strode to the corkboard, and began to make notes on my index-card time line, hoping to forestall the talking-to I knew Julia was about to give me. My hope was in vain.

"Rachel Stowe, you are a stubborn woman. What did you expect the chief to say? He's got a job to do. Should he neglect his duties just to please your highness?"

Holly's eyes shifted from Julia's to mine. "What happened? Tell me."

"Jenny Hannaford complained to Chief Gilroy about Rachel questioning her, so doing his *job*"—Julia punctuated the word with a finger wag aimed at me—"he told Rachel not to talk to her anymore."

"He mentioned a restraining order, Holly. The word *imperious* comes to mind."

"You weren't taking him seriously and he needed to get your attention," Julia said.

"I talked to him, didn't I? That's all he's entitled to. Now can we please get on with this?" I waved my hands at the corkboard. No way was I going to let James Gilroy distract me. I'd seen the way he'd charmed Jenny. He did it with every woman. Him and his blue eyes. He'd even done it with Julia, smiling and offering her his seat.

I dropped to my chair again and tried to banish such ugly thoughts. I'd seen nothing in Gilroy's character to suggest he was a con man—or enjoyed strutting his stuff in order to prop up his ego. I hadn't even seen his face when he'd talked to Jenny. All I'd seen was Jenny's schoolgirl reaction—her twirling her hair. And now I was punishing him for being kind to Julia. It was time to get a grip on myself.

Truth was, I had pushed him away at the first silly

opportunity because along with his beautiful eyes, I'd seen goodness in him and assumed he could never be interested in the likes of me—no matter what Underhill thought. And now, after my outrageous behavior, I was almost certainly right.

"You tell him, Holly," I repeated. "He should know. We can't keep discoveries from him."

My friends were wise enough to read the tone of my voice and know the subject was closed.

"Gilroy or Underhill stops by the bakery first thing most mornings. I'll tell one of them then," Holly said.

"Fantastic information, though," I said, forcing a lighter tone into my voice.

"I thought you'd like it."

"Now we need to find out which friend Maureen was meeting. Then we've got our killer."

"I think we can write off Kirk as a suspect now," Holly said. "If he'd killed her, he would have burned her journal."

Julia huffed—along with her nudging, she'd been doing that a lot lately—and sat in one of the room's wooden chairs, resigned to moving on from the subject of Chief Gilroy. "How do we intend to find out which friend she was meeting?"

"I'm sure if the flash drive could be traced, Gilroy would have by now," Holly said. "Same for the printout with the riddle on it."

It struck me again that the killer had gone to a lot of trouble, when he or she could simply have stabbed Maureen as she passed by. With all the scavengers milling about, the killer could have done the deed and disappeared into the crowd before Maureen hit the sidewalk. And that method had the added benefit of not leaving a flash drive behind for the police to discover. "I wonder about that riddle. Writing it was a risky thing to do, and so was planting a flash drive. Why not sneak up on Maureen or have her wait in the Andersons' yard for the drive?"

"Because the riddle and drive were fun and they annoyed Maureen," Julia said.

Holly and I turned in unison. Of course. Not everything was a convoluted clue. Some questions found their answers in the personality of the murderer.

"You're absolutely right," I said. Trouble was, every single one of Maureen's chums and rivals from her high school days wanted to annoy her. And she them.

"But that doesn't narrow down the field of suspects," Holly said. "I've never seen people so unwilling to let the past be the past. The funny thing is, they've all got great lives in Juniper Grove, and they chose to stay here. Most of them married, they own businesses, Olivia just became president of the Juniper Grove Development Association."

"I still think something out of the ordinary happened recently," I said. "Something brand new. That's what we need to focus on. High school only explains their obsessive behavior, not how their obsession turned to murder."

"What about the vote for presidency of the JGDA?" Holly asked.

"Maybe that's part of it," I replied, "but I can't picture it as the only reason. There's something more, something bigger."

"What about feeding meat to Jenny?" Holly said. "For vegetarians, eating meat must be like eating roadkill."

"Oh, Holly!" Julia cried.

"Or that pumpkin-carving contest," Holly said. "Cheating Justin out of a third championship in a row."

"I'm putting my money on an affair," Julia said. "Rachel and I saw Jenny and Justin hugging outside the Town Hall."

"With Tyler standing right there," I reminded her.

"It was a very long hug."

"But it wasn't passionate, it was . . . sympathetic." I'd been trying to put another label on Jenny's hug and the expression on Tyler's face since seeing them after the meeting. Something beyond "deep friendship." Now I knew why I had immediately dismissed thoughts of an affair. There had been no spark in Jenny's embrace, no hint of jealousy from Tyler. Though it was possible Jenny was just a good actress. She certainly was dramatic.

Holly wandered to the window and pulled back the drapes on one side.

"It's late for you. Go home," I said.

"My mind's racing."

"Get a good night's sleep and we'll see you in the morning," Julia said.

Holly let the drape fall. "You know the kid who wrote 'Murderer' on my window?" She swung back to us. "His name is Matt. His parents brought him by the bakery today so he could apologize to me again. They apologized again too, and I felt so sorry for them. They strike me as good people."

"I'm glad to hear that," Julia said.

"It was after school, so Caleb was in back by the ovens. After Matt's parents left, I sent him in the back so Caleb could show him what needs to be cleaned and when, since he's starting work here this Saturday. I don't know what I expected. Shouting, maybe. But about ten minutes later I heard them laughing. I peeked around the door, and there they were, laughing about something that had happened at school. You would have thought they were friends."

"Maybe they will be," I said.

"After today I wouldn't be surprised," Holly said. "It's strange, isn't it? Why is it that Matt and Caleb can make up and move on, and Justin, Tyler, and the rest couldn't? What's the difference?"

CHAPTER 15

Needless to say, I didn't solve Maureen's murder overnight, but Holly's information set me on a new path. After breakfast, I drove downtown and parked across the street from Blooms. I intended to put Olivia's mind at ease over Gina's windows—and then take the opportunity to ask her again what she remembered from the night of the scavenger hunt. Maybe guilt over hiring thugs to break Gina's windows would grease the wheels of her memory.

I stepped out of my car and looked across Main Street. The windows in Olivia's shop, which at first I thought were dark in a trick of the morning light, I now realized were missing. And outside on the sidewalk, Officer Underhill was taking photos. I sprinted across the street, just ahead of four cars—a traffic jam by Juniper Grove standards. The tempered glass of the shop windows had shattered into a thousand glass pebbles, sparkling in the bright sunshine on the sidewalk and peppering the display platform just inside the store.

"What happened?" I asked Underhill.

"Do you turn up at all the window breakings?" he said with a grin.

"I guess I'm just lucky that way. Did this happen last night?"

"Yup. The owner discovered it when she opened the

125

store."

"What on earth is going on?"

"That's about what Gilroy said." He leaned toward me and said under his breath, "This is what they call payback."

"You're not suggesting Gina Peeler had anything to do with this?"

"Maybe someone who wants to defend her after what happened to her house."

"That would be a lot of people. Is it okay if I go in?"

"Now you're asking me?"

I headed inside, leaving Underhill's question unanswered. Underhill was okay most of the time, but there was a side to him—a side that seemed to be growing now that his duties had doubled with the departure of the department's third officer in September—that took easy offense when he thought his officer-ness was being challenged in any way, however small. Maybe that kind of attitude worked in a big city, but not Juniper Grove, where people saw the police force as a genuine part of the community.

When Olivia saw me, she sprang from her stool behind the register and cut across the store. "Thanks a lot, Rachel. You and your big mouth."

Gilroy was fast behind her.

"If you hadn't said anything," Olivia went on, "this wouldn't have happened. I can't believe you!"

Gilroy thrust out his arm, jamming it between Olivia and me like a boxing referee trying to halt a fight. "Mrs. Seitz, this has nothing to do with Miss Stowe."

Olivia turned on him. "It has everything to do with her. She accused me in full hearing of Gina Peeler and your other officer of hiring kids to break Gina's windows."

126

Gilroy stared. "Which is what you did."

"That's not the point."

Puzzled, Gilroy scratched the back of his head. "Then I'm not getting the point."

"It should have been kept private!" Olivia screeched. "I was willing to admit to it, but I didn't want the whole town to know. I just became president of the Juniper Grove Development Association. How do you think it looks for me to have hired them? Huh? How?"

The words were on the tip of my tongue: *You should have thought of that beforehand*. But I said nothing. Gilroy's answer was more diplomatic than my thoughts.

"This is a small town, and people would have found out eventually," he said. "Best to get it out now. It'll be old news in a month."

Olivia spent a moment in silent glowering, probably wondering whether she should let loose with another screech. But instead she grumbled, "In the meantime, I have to deal with this destruction. I have to pay for this *and* Gina's windows. My insurance company will refuse to renew my policy."

"It's possible this has nothing to do with Gina Peeler," Gilroy said. "Let's not assume."

"Are you out of your mind? You can't make a simple, logical connection between that event and this and you want me to believe you're smart enough to find out who did this?" Olivia said.

Ignoring the barb, Gilroy tried again to soothe Olivia. "These crimes can be difficult to solve, but I'll do my best."

"Unfortunately, your best isn't close to good enough." Olivia executed a sharp pivot and headed back to the safety of her stool.

Underhill, who had been hiding in a corner of the store while Olivia raged, approached Gilroy, told him he needed to get another memory card from the station, and quickly exited the store.

Gilroy continued to work the scene, talking to Olivia with gentleness and respect, as though she hadn't just insulted him. Watching him, I understood as never before that I was wrong in thinking he was cold and reserved. On the contrary, he was calm and judicious, qualities necessary in a police chief. Surviving encounters with people like Olivia demanded that he be. And to think that yesterday I'd added to the sort of guff he had to put up with. The question was, what was he like off the job? Far from the pressures of work, would the cool, calm Gilroy remain?

When Gilroy looked my way, I turned my attention to the shop floor, to three large rocks that had been hurled through the windows and to the tiny bits of glass sparkling like rough-cut diamonds. And a shining silver bangle in the midst of them.

"Do you need something, Rachel?" Gilroy said, heading my way.

I waited until he drew closer so I could point at the floor without Olivia seeing. "I might be completely, utterly wrong, but that looks like one of Jenny Hannaford's bangles."

"We were waiting for Underhill to take photos in here. You can't be sure?"

"I don't know anyone else who wears four or six silver bangles on her arm. Did Olivia see this?"

"Yes."

I took his silence after that to mean that Olivia hadn't identified the bangle as Jenny's, or even suggested it might

128

be hers. "I saw Olivia talking to Tyler Hannaford yesterday, and so did Jenny. Something about them talking bothered her. I wonder if—"

"Where was this?"

"Jenny, Julia, and I were on the sidewalk on this side of the street, and Olivia and Tyler were across the street. Just about where my car was parked, if you remember."

"I remember."

"I wonder if Jenny threw those rocks and her bangle came off in the process."

"Should be easy enough to find out if it's hers." He paused and gave his chin a slow scratch. "Listen, I have to ask you to leave. We haven't even bagged the evidence."

"Of course, sorry." I was about to make my exit when I remembered Maureen's journal. "There's one more thing. Have you talked to Holly at the bakery this morning?"

"No, why?"

"Kirk Nicholson found Maureen's journal, and in it she wrote she was going to meet an old friend during the scavenger hunt. This friend was supposed to give her information she could use against another old friend."

"When did he find this?"

"Yesterday. He happened to mention it to Holly. He hadn't had a chance to tell you yet. So Holly was going to tell you, and then . . ."

I stopped jabbering. Gilroy had gotten the picture. I'd been meddling again.

"Okay, thanks," he said.

A few derisive words came to mind. I bit my tongue.

"You're going to have to leave now, Rachel."

"All right. Just thought you'd want to know."

"It was helpful. Thank you."

129

"Good. I'm glad to help. Really, I am. If I can help again, just let me know."

Negotiating the minefield of broken glass at my feet, I made it to the sidewalk as fast as humanly possible. What did he think of me? That I was trying to take over his job or show him up? That, like Olivia, I thought he was stupid? I stood at the curb, grimacing and rubbing my temples as if to rub away the stupidness that popped up whenever I was in James Gilroy's presence.

I wheeled back to face Blooms. Underhill had returned with his new memory card and was inside the store by the broken windows, gaping at me and wondering, I suspected, if I was experiencing the onset of a migraine. Gilroy was talking to Olivia again, calming her.

Who was this man, this anomaly? Who talked like him anymore? Acted like him? Oh, I was falling for him. A police chief. A man who made me nervous and had me blathering like a teenager. Not that it mattered. It seemed clear that Gilroy had had just about enough of me.

"Are you all right, Miss Stowe?" Underhill called.

I waved at him. "Fine. Just wondering where to go next." Figuratively, anyway. Literally, I knew exactly where I was going next. I hopped into my car and drove east to the Porter Grill. I didn't know if Justin would be willing to talk again, but it was worth a try. There were questions about Maureen that only he could answer.

Though the restaurant didn't officially open until ten o'clock in the morning, the front door was unlocked when I arrived. I wandered inside, my eyes adjusting to the dimmer indoor lighting, and soon saw Justin and what I supposed was his chef at a back booth.

Not wanting to intrude any more than I already had, I

stood still and said his name.

"Give me two minutes," he answered.

I slid into a booth near the front door to wait for him. I'd half expected an angry response to my interruption, but he appeared more resigned than anything else, figuring, I thought, that he would have to put up with me until Maureen's killer was found.

The chef slid out from the booth, and Justin, moving at a slower pace, worked his way to the end of his seat and pushed himself to his feet. If he was this tired before lunch, how tired was he at the end of dinner service?

He ambled over to my booth, angled his body, and dropped to the edge of the opposite seat. "More questions?" he asked.

His face was gaunt, ashen. I thought of Holly and how the stress of running a bakery might show on her face in five years' time. "Do you mind?"

"No, not really. I'd like this whole thing to be over, and whether it's you or our police chief who settles things, I don't care."

"It'll be Chief Gilroy," I said, "but if I can help him, I will."

"Then shoot."

"What can you tell me about Maureen in her high school days? Were you friends, or was she an outsider back then too?"

"If you go back far enough, we were friends. We even dated a few times, and I took her to the senior prom."

"I heard you got into an argument."

Justin looked past me to a distant point over my shoulder. When he looked back and spoke, I heard regret in his voice. "We sure did. A rip-roaring fight that lasted most of the night. It started when we weren't elected prom king and queen. She told me she'd tried to get me to 'smarten up' so we could win. She was competitive even then. And being a kid, I didn't take it very well. I'd already decided to break up with her, and that sealed it. And then Olivia . . ."

"Yes?"

"Olivia was a senior too, so she felt left out. So did Tyler and Jenny. You have to understand, we were all close back then. All for one and one for all. When one of us went somewhere, the others had to be there. They were jealous. I was graduating, and it was like I was taking Maureen with me, but not them." He spread his hands across the table. "I wasn't. Instead, I was breaking up with her, but that isn't what Maureen told them. She lorded it over them. 'I'm going to hang around Justin and you aren't.'"

"How did they react?"

"Somehow they got hold of her prom dress and cut the stitching on it. Just enough so when she danced the stitching began to unravel in the back. She didn't feel it at first, and the fabric pulled apart. She wasn't wearing a slip, so . . . People started snickering and pointing. It was bad."

It was more than bad, I wanted to say. It was just about the worst thing that could happen to a high school sophomore at her first big dance with her boyfriend.

"I laughed, like a jerk," Justin said. "I apologized later, but she didn't want to hear about it."

"Did the others apologize to her?"

"No. After that we didn't see her much until a few years later."

I leaned back, mulling over what Justin had said, picturing the incident with the dress and the effect it must have had on a young girl infatuated with an older boy. "Do you think Maureen's resentment goes back to that prom?"

"I've wondered about that, but how could it? It was a terrible thing for them to do, and it was wrong for me to laugh, but that was more than twenty years ago. I can't imagine her holding on to that all these years. Besides . . ."

Again he hesitated. This time I had to pry it out of him. "If you think it's important, speak up. This has gone on long enough."

He nodded. It was time. "Maureen didn't hate me. Two weeks ago she came into my restaurant and told me she still loved me. She said we'd make a great pair now that she'd opened her own business. She thought I'd see her differently after she opened Coffee and Cakes. I honestly think that's why she started the business."

So Maureen's flame had never quite died. Or she had rekindled it in the face of her upcoming divorce. "Can I ask what you said?"

"I said I didn't feel the same way. I told her I knew what she'd done to Jenny at the vegetarian dinner and how she'd threatened Tyler's job at the Spruce Tavern, among other things. Then I told her I wanted her to move on, and I hoped she'd have a good life with her husband."

CHAPTER 16

"It's not that I don't feel sorry for her," Holly said as she wiped down the top of the pastry display case with a lemon-scented cloth, "but to hold on to such anger for so long is crazy. When I was her age, I would have been furious and embarrassed to death for a few months, and I hate to say this, but I probably would have tried to get back at them, but I would have let it go."

"She didn't, and look what happened to her," I said.

"You stay angry that long and you can make yourself sick."

"I don't think she ever told Kirk what happened. He would have mentioned it to me."

"If that had happened to me, I wouldn't have told Peter. I'd bury it deep in the past."

"It makes you think, doesn't it? One event, sad but not earth-shattering, and more than twenty years later someone dies because of it. And then there's the broken windows. Did you hear Olivia had her shop windows broken?"

"I hear everything." Holly dropped the cloth into a bin under the display case and pulled a fresh one from a plastic container. "This place is Juniper Grove's Grand Central Station. Anyway, Officer Underhill came in later than usual today and I pried it out of him."

I told Holly about Jenny's reaction to seeing Olivia

chatting with Tyler, and about finding the silver bangle in Blooms. "I think Jenny did it. When she threw a rock, the bangle slipped off and went through the broken window."

"Julia told me about Jenny's meltdown at the vegetarian dinner," said Holly, who was focusing her cleaning wrath on the inside of her microwave. "I guess anyone who can throw a ramekin at a wall can throw a rock at a window. She needs help."

"They all need help. The only one of them who has half a brain is Justin. I think he's genuinely sorry he hurt Maureen—and he only laughed at her, he didn't plan the dress thing. But Maureen accepted his apology. More than accepted."

Holly stopped scrubbing and turned around.

"Justin said that Maureen came to him two weeks ago and told him she still loves him. He told her no."

"Wow."

"After all these years."

"You found the new information you were looking for."

"Maybe." Before I could elaborate, a young couple entered the bakery and made a beeline for the pain au chocolat. I took a seat at one of Holly's small tables and worked my way through the facts, wondering if Justin's rejection of Maureen was indeed the brand-new piece of the puzzle I'd been searching for. Maureen had been vindictive before, feeding Jenny beef, threatening Tyler's job at the Spruce Tavern, and running for president of the JGDA against her old friends, but when Justin turned her down and told her to go back to her husband, she went on a rampage, trying to destroy his restaurant, Olivia's store, and even Holly's bakery, probably because Holly and Justin got along.

She even went so far as to cheat in a pumpkin-carving contest to spite Justin and to accuse Caleb of throwing eggs at her house. Petty things, but Maureen went big *and* small. It made no difference to her. It was all sweet revenge.

Was that why one of them killed her? To put an end to her escalating attacks? Maybe, but that didn't tell me *who* had killed her. Every single one of them had reason to, and all of them, as far as I could guess, were capable. They'd been pushed to their limits, and even with Maureen gone, the bond of their friendship had been strained. In the aftermath of her death, they had become irrational, suspecting each other, hurting each other. If Olivia found out—and she would—that it was probably Jenny who had broken her windows, what might happen next?

At least Holly wasn't in danger. I hadn't said anything to her, but for a while I'd worried that she was being framed. No longer. The killer had taken the drive from Maureen's hand and dropped it into an open backpack pocket, hoping that whoever owned the backpack would carry it from the scene. And by now Gilroy, even most of Juniper Grove, knew for certain Holly wasn't a killer. The danger came from and threatened only three people. The fourth was the murderer. Maureen, who had scavenged for gossip to hurt those who had hurt her so very long ago, wasn't the only threat to the once tight-knit band.

Wearing big smiles and bearing two pink pastry boxes, the lucky devils, the couple exited the store.

"I forgot to tell you Chief Gilroy stopped by too," Holly said. "Thanks for letting him know what Kirk told me."

"No problem. Feel like going with me and Julia to the Spruce Tavern for an early dinner?"

Holly wrinkled her nose. "They have food?"

"Pretty good food, by the sound of it. Pub style."

"This has a purpose, I take it?"

"Finding Maureen's killer."

"Oh, shoot." Holly snapped her fingers. "I can't. We're having dinner with Michael and Emily Ward, Matt's parents.

"How wonderful!"

"Night before last we were glaring at each other across the lobby of the police station. You know, it was Gilroy who set us on the right track."

"Don't start."

"I'm not Julia. What you do or don't do when it comes to Gilroy is your business. I'm just saying he's a good guy, and good guys are hard to come by. I think I got one of the last ones."

I looked to the door, making sure what I was about to say would be private. There was no one at the door, no one on the sidewalk. Even so, I whispered. "Holly, he's not interested in me. I like him, but I'm not his type."

"Stop it, you—"

"And I think I blew any chance I had when I acted like a brat yesterday. Julia said I hurt his feelings."

"He's not that fragile."

Suddenly I felt the need to talk about Gilroy. I wanted Holly to ask me what he'd said and what I'd said, word for word, so I could explain myself. Not that I had a sterling explanation for my bratty words, but I felt the need to tell her that I was falling for the man, and it was *because* I was falling for him that I was acting like a teenager. But she didn't ask, and I let it drop. "I guess he can't be fragile, considering his line of work."

"I knew you liked him from the start. I could tell."

137

"Could you? I didn't do something stupid like flip my hair, did I?"

"What?" Holly laughed.

"Though I can't really flip mine. It's not thick enough, and there's that weird cowlick at the back."

"You have a great smile."

"Gee, thanks. Do you know if he's ever been married?"

Holly seemed stumped by the question. "I don't know. Funny, but I've never thought about it. He seems so . . ."

"Intensely single?" I offered.

"Now you're trying to talk yourself out of going for him."

"It's not up to me, Holly."

"Well, give it a think. Don't dismiss him before you've done that."

"I won't."

I left the bakery—without a pink box of my own—and strolled west on Main Street, mulling over Maureen's murder. Holly and Caleb were going to be okay, but the old high school gang was in danger, and I wanted more than anything to prove to Gilroy that I wasn't just a meddler. Now my task was to convince Julia to go with me to the Spruce Tavern this evening. Loud Celtic bands in a pub setting weren't her thing, but I needed to talk to Tyler. Back at Juniper Grove High, he'd been the odd man out, a tag-along. Maureen, Olivia, and Jenny had wanted Justin, and they had made no secret of it. Like Maureen, Tyler had been a sophomore at the time of the prom, and I couldn't help but think that played a part in his wanting to humiliate Maureen by sabotaging her dress.

Storm clouds were gathering over the mountains. Soon they would spill into the foothills and then down over

Juniper Grove. The air was rich with the scent of fallen leaves and ripe grass, growing lush after the recent rains. Outside the doors at Grove Coffee, an employee was sweeping leaves from around the shop's jack-o'-lanterns, fat orange globes on either side of the door, and across the street, another employee, dressed as a scarecrow, was offering candy to passersby.

Tomorrow was October 31, but there wasn't going to be any Halloween in Juniper Grove. As Julia had so succinctly pointed out, parents weren't going to send their kids out trick-or-treating with a knife-wielding killer on the loose. Feeling the cold and damp, I raised the zipper on my jacket. My favorite, teal-colored jacket. Though I'd had it cleaned, I could still see the ghost of blueberry on it, where a glob of jelly-donut filling had landed seconds before I'd run into James Gilroy on the sidewalk. Julia said the jacket was perfectly clean and I was imagining things.

Thinking a little caffeine was in order, I turned about and headed back to Grove Coffee, following the aroma of fresh-brewed coffee through the door and up to the bar. Waiting for my turn to order, I glanced about me, looking for familiar faces, and glimpsed Justin and Tyler at a two-seat table by the window. Somehow I had to wheedle my way into their conversation, even if I had to hover over them.

I ordered a caramel macchiato and walked as nonchalantly as possible to their table. Tyler straightened his spine and raised his chin as I approached, waiting for me to speak. At that moment, he reminded me of Officer Underhill—ready to pounce if I even bent the social rules, which, judging by his demeanor, he thought I already had.

"Hi, guys, nice to see you here. Mind if I join you?"

"There are only two chairs," Tyler groused.

"There's one behind you," Justin said, tossing his head at the empty table directly behind me. I dragged over a chair and sat, smiling as though meeting them had made my day. Neither of them had stood or helped me with the chair, so social rules were out the window.

"Justin, I thought you'd be at the restaurant this time of day," I said.

"I'm taking a break," he said. His skin was pasty, nearly translucent, and his voice was raw, as if he'd just tumbled out of bed.

"You seem tired," I said.

Tyler made a puffing sound and shifted in his seat.

"Tyler, Julia and I are coming to the Spruce Tavern tonight. I've heard such good things about it." I hadn't asked Julia yet, but the tension at the table was palpable, and I was desperate to fill the silence.

"You've never been there?"

"I've been wanting to since I moved here. You know how it is. It takes awhile to get around to things."

"I think you'll like it," Tyler said. "We've got a great band tonight." He angled his head and squinted at me, and I saw in his eyes a warning. When he turned back to Justin, his expression softened. "I need to go."

"I'm good," Justin said.

Tyler rose to his feet, a simple action he infused with a great deal of drama. "Let me know if you need a ride later."

"Right," Justin replied.

Tyler left Grove Coffee, but not without eyeballing me over his shoulder. That warning look again. I claimed Tyler's vacated chair. "Did I say something wrong?"

Justin took a tissue from his jeans pocket, worked it against his nose, and then pushed it back into his pocket.

"Tyler's a good friend, but he's a little overprotective on my bad days."

"Your bad days?"

Justin's tongue passed over his pale, dry lips. "Today is one of the bad days. I can't even smell my coffee."

I glanced at his cup. He had barely touched it. I was beginning to understand. The tiredness, the pale skin—even the bald head, which I thought he'd shaved in a nod to current fashion. "Are you sick, Justin?"

"Hopefully I won't be a few months from now, but right now?" He smiled weakly. "Chemotherapy is worse than the disease it's supposed to cure."

CHAPTER 17

Julia and I found the perfect seat for observing all the action at the Spruce Tavern. It was in a corner, with a good view of the other tables, the bar, and the stage on which the band, the Edinburgh Aces, was playing a raucous tune, much to Julia's horror. "Look at it this way," I said, leaning close, "no one can hear what we're saying."

"Including us," she mouthed.

"Try the bacon and brie sandwich," I shouted, pointing at the menu. "That's what I'm getting. I'll bet it's good."

I'm pretty sure Julia grunted. That's what it sounded like, anyway. I took it to mean that the tavern's sandwich selection wasn't to her liking, and her tightly pursed lips supported my translation.

"What on earth kind of food is this?" she said, leaning my way. "Where are the ham sandwiches and cheeseburgers?" She tossed the menu to the table. "I'll have a beer."

"You?" I said with a laugh.

"There's nothing wrong with a glass of beer in the evening."

"I know, it's just that I've never seen you drink beer."

"Prepare to be astonished."

Using what must have been superhuman hearing, a waiter took our order, asked Julia if she was sure she didn't want chips or something, and then trotted back to the bar. I was about to shout at Julia again when the band ground to a sudden halt and announced, to scattered applause, a fifteen-minute break. Julia breathed a sigh of relief. "Oh, they've stopped. Blessed silence."

"There's Tyler," I said, directing her attention to the stage. "He's talking to the band."

Checking to see that no one was in earshot, Julia said, "What do you think of him as a murderer?"

"Unfortunately, the same thing I think of all of them. He has motivation and he's capable."

"But you don't think Justin is."

"Not now I don't. He doesn't have the strength to kill anyone. You should have seen him."

"But the murder happened Monday and this is Friday. He might have had his strength then."

She had a point. And driving a knife into someone *was* more of a male thing. Women killed with poison. But although Justin, Tyler, and Olivia had suffered the most at Maureen's hands, having their livelihoods threatened, only Olivia had retaliated. She'd chosen the wrong person to get even with, but her revenge had been supreme. Threaten me with the Health Department? I'll break every window in your house.

On the other hand, Jenny had taken revenge to a new level by breaking Olivia's windows. If she could do that to a friend, killing Maureen would have been easy. And Tyler? He'd wanted to throttle me just for talking to his sick friend. I scanned the crowded tavern for Jenny and Olivia but didn't see either of them. Tyler was doing well. Far better than Justin at the Porter Grill, in fact.

"Tyler," Julia said, kicking me under the table.

"Hey, there," Tyler said, sauntering up to our table. "Listen, Rachel." Without asking, probably thinking turnabout was fair play, he worked his way around the table and took the open chair with a direct line of sight to the bar. Giving me a crooked smile, he said, "Justin said I was kinda rude this afternoon. I didn't realize. Sorry. He said he told you about his chemo."

"Yeah, he did," I said, "and it's fine, Tyler, I understand. You were trying to keep me from tiring him out."

"Thanks." He sank back in his seat. "He's going through a rough time."

"Did he have chemo today?"

"No, he has it every Monday. He's really sick on Monday and Tuesdays, but he's run down all week. He's still trying to keep the restaurant going."

No wonder he wasn't at the scavenger hunt on Monday, I thought. That settled it. Justin was too ill to play games with riddles and flash drives, lure Maureen into the Andersons' yard, and then stab her. My field of suspects had dwindled to three.

Tyler's eyes slipped past me to a point somewhere behind my chair. He stiffened, and I jerked my head around. Jenny stood two feet from me.

"Tyler, you're supposed to be working," she said. "What are we going to do if you get fired?"

"I'm talking with the clientele," he said.

"You're talking to women. Again. You're not—"

"You're not my employer," he growled, "so stop acting like it. I don't come to your work and tell you what to do."

"That's because I'm not the one messing things up!"

"Get my off my back, Jenny."

144

"What did you just say?" Jenny's eyebrows arched, and the whites of her eyes shone around her irises. I had a feeling we were about to witness another Night of the Ramekins.

"Jenny, he was answering my questions," I said. The expression on her face made me shut my mouth.

"Rachel Stowe, you may be single, but that's your own fault. Stay away from my husband. Trust me, you're not that appealing."

I could give as good as I got, jab for verbal jab, but I wasn't interested in that. After witnessing what petty grievances and retaliation had done to Jenny and her friends, revenge, even on a small and swift scale, was of no interest to me. "I'm not trying to steal Tyler, and I'm sorry you got that impression."

Jenny swung at my water glass, whacking it and sending it flying toward the next table.

"Enough!" Tyler shouted, thumping the table.

Someone must have cued the band, because the instant Tyler smacked the table, it started up—almost but not quite swamping Jenny's howls of indignation. Tyler scrambled from his seat, grabbed her by the hand, and hauled her to an open door behind the bar. A second later the door slammed shut.

While a waiter picked up pieces of shattered glass, the unfortunate target of my glass, a woman one table over, mopped water from her jacket with the help of her friends. I mouthed the word "Sorry" and she mouthed back, "No problem."

Julia couldn't tear her eyes from the door. "I've never seen such anger over nothing," she yelled. "What did she mean stay away from her husband?"

"She thought I was after Tyler." I swallowed a smile. This wasn't a time to laugh, but Jenny had to be on another planet to think I was having a fling with her husband.

"There's your killer," Julia said.

I cupped my hands around my ears.

"I said, Jenny Hannaford is your killer."

Hearing Julia—and almost everyone could hear her—the people at the next table froze. Julia must have felt their eyes on her, because she swiveled in her seat a little and waved at them, smiling sweetly.

Pushing my plate out of the way, I leaned toward her. "Maybe this wasn't a good idea. Should we go?"

"I thought you'd never ask."

I left a twenty for the tab and tip, weaved my way around the tables toward the door, and stepped into the chilly night air.

Outside on the sidewalk, Julia tugged on an earlobe. "My ears are ringing. Tell me again why we came?"

"Do you hear that?"

"I can't hear anything."

Turning around, I saw Justin hobbling his way up the sidewalk toward me. He stopped, steadied himself with his hand on a brick wall, and heaved for breath.

"Justin, what are you doing?" I said, hurrying to him. "You should be resting."

"Oh, yeah," he managed, continuing to gasp for breath. "But we need to talk."

I looked around for a bench or even a low retaining wall to sit on.

"Get your car," Julia commanded.

"I'm just out of breath," Justin said. "Out of shape. Just give me a sec."

146

I ignored him and darted back up the block for my Forester. When I drove back, I was able to pull to the curb feet from where he stood. He waited for Julia to get in the front seat before he clambered in the back.

"I'm glad I caught you before you went home," he said.

Sideways in our seats, our necks craned to the back, Julia and I watched him as his breath slowed and his color returned.

"I've been thinking about something I heard," he said. "It's been bothering me, and I thought you should know. When we were in my restaurant, Jenny told you that Maureen asked to be part of Team Main Street for the scavenger hunt. But that's not true. It was the other way around. I was with Jenny, Olivia, and Tyler in the Porter Grill when they asked Maureen to join them. It was their idea."

"How devious," Julia said.

"It started me thinking," Justin said. "Why would they lie about that? It's not like they had to. Who cares who asked who?"

For a moment I couldn't speak. I didn't like what I was beginning to think. I didn't like it one bit.

I thanked Justin and told him I would drive him back to his restaurant, and despite his protestations, I did, pulling from the curb before he could get out. His health seemed more precarious than he was willing to admit. I glanced at him in my rearview mirror, his head tilted back, his eyes closed.

I found an open spot near the restaurant door—not a good sign on a Friday night—and nosed in. "We're here." I threw my right arm over the seat back and faced Justin. "Do you mind if I ask you one more question?"

"Go for it."

"Did you change your menu at the Porter Grill for health reasons?"

"Soon after I was diagnosed. I heard a vegetarian diet can help, and I thought, why not? I'll give it a try. Since I eat my meals at the restaurant, I thought I'd add some vegetarian dishes to the menu, and maybe others would like them too." He shrugged.

"Was it Jenny who suggested the change?"

"Yeah, it was. She brought in the recipes and even talked to my chef. She helps Tyler come up with dishes for the Spruce, but I've taken her away from that lately. Taken up all her time. She's been amazing." He put his hand on the door handle. "In retrospect it wasn't a great idea. I don't mean the vegetarian food—I like it now—I mean changing the menu at the restaurant. Porter Grill customers like their steak and potatoes. I'm going to have to go back to that if I don't want the doors to close."

"What will Jenny say?"

"She doesn't care as long as *I* eat vegetarian." He chuckled. "She can be a little too helpful, if you know what I mean. She's sweet, but she's a worrier."

"Maybe have just one vegetarian dish on the menu?" I said.

"That's an idea."

"But not tofu," Julia said. "Please, nothing with tofu in it."

"That's Olivia coming this way," Justin said.

He stayed inside the car and made no move to wave down his friend or catch her eye. I turned around and faced front as Olivia approached, stopped, and stared intently through my windshield.

148

"I don't mean this as a judgment on you, Justin, but your friends can be very rude," Julia said.

I'd had enough. I popped open the car door and threw a leg outside, startling Olivia to her senses.

"Rachel, I, I . . ."

"Olivia?"

"Sorry to stare. My mind is elsewhere."

"Who is it you're surprised to see?"

"What do you mean?"

"Are you worried about what Justin might say? Little things he might remember?"

In a last effort to appear in command, she put her hands on her hips and gave me a smug smile. "Boy, you are nuts, lady."

"All those little clues, little pieces of the puzzle."

"You need to go home and get some rest." She looked to the sky as it began to drizzle.

"You know that blue stationery I bought at your store? The shade of blue was called Robin's Egg."

Her hands fell to her side. An icy moment of silence followed.

"It's just another clue, not very meaningful on its own," I went on. "Remember the riddle found in Maureen's hand? 'Blue like a robin's egg.' Most people would have called it blue. Just blue. But then, most people wouldn't write a riddle. They'd just hand over the flash drive."

Seeking Justin's help, she shot a bewildered look at the car. He remained inside, but I'd left the car door open, and I was certain he was hearing every word. Maybe it was the traffic on the street and the customers coming out of restaurants and milling about on the sidewalks that gave me an undue sense of safety, or maybe I was anxious to prove

149

myself to Gilroy, but I decided to tell Olivia what I knew—and to give her a chance to explain herself so Gilroy could keep another one of the old Juniper High gang from dying.

"When did you realize things had gone wrong? Please tell me it was after Maureen was murdered."

Olivia sucked in her breath, and in a small voice, she said, "It wasn't supposed to happen that way."

CHAPTER 18

We stood in the drizzle, Olivia's perfectly cropped bangs wet against her head, and stared each other down. She told me she'd deny everything if I spoke a word of what she was saying to Chief Gilroy. I could tell she wanted to ease her conscience, but she knew if she confirmed my suspicions, she would betray a decades-old friendship and implicate herself in a crime. It seemed to me that the latter was more important to her.

"Did you mean for it to go this far?" I asked.

"No, never."

"When did you realize things had gone wrong?"

"Only when I saw Maureen. I couldn't believe my eyes. At first I was sure someone else killed her. There was a waiting list for all the people who wanted to murder that woman."

"Then you put the pieces together and knew Jenny did it."

Olivia nodded.

"And knowing that, you still didn't say anything to Chief Gilroy?"

She shook her head.

"You knew Jenny could kill again."

"She wouldn't."

"She might kill you."

Olivia scrunched up her face. "Don't be ridiculous. We're friends."

I couldn't help but laugh. "From what I've seen, it doesn't take much to set her off. Friend, husband—it doesn't matter to her. Look what she did to your shop windows because she saw you talking to Tyler. I'll bet you recognized her bangle on the ground before Chief Gilroy even showed it to you."

She lifted a shoulder and issued a noncommittal mumble.

"Tonight in the Spruce Tavern Jenny screamed like a banshee at Tyler for talking to me."

"Jenny thinks every woman is after her husband." Olivia chortled, amused by the absurdity of the idea. "I was talking to him yesterday because he was beginning to believe Jenny had killed Maureen. He remembered that she left us at the first checkpoint when she said there was someone she wanted to talk to. Tyler thought she might have run into Justin, but he found out later how sick he was that night. Then he saw her gloves in the kitchen trash can."

"Did he pull them out? Did he save them?"

"Of course not, Rachel. He didn't want to know why they were in there. Not right away."

"And when he came to you, you tried to talk him out of his suspicions?"

"I couldn't let him think that about Jenny."

"Because he'd turn her in, and then Jenny would turn you in, and what a legal pickle that would be."

She flung out her forefinger, aiming it at me. "Tyler and I were only trying to get Maureen to back off. We didn't know what Jenny was going to do."

"But all three of you asked her to join Team Main

Street so you could lure her into the Andersons' yard the night of the scavenger hunt. Did you hand her the riddle about the flash drive?"

"At the first checkpoint. I stuck it in her hand and told her to go to the Andersons' front yard."

"What juicy gossip did you promise her?"

"We told her it was about Justin. That's what she wanted. But we couldn't be seen giving her the drive, so we had to do it with the scavenger hunt as cover. Besides, the whole arrangement was right up her alley. All that cloak and dagger. She bought it. She would have bought anything to get back at Justin."

It sickened me that Olivia was proud of her deceit, even knowing it had ended in murder. "And once you got her to the Andersons' yard, what were you going to do to her? It's not as if you could sabotage her prom dress again."

Olivia flinched at my last words, and for a moment I saw how miserable she was and how she regretted the past, though more for her own sake than Maureen's.

"Maureen could never let that go," she said softly. "All these years and she's as angry now as she was then. Can we get out of the rain?"

As we climbed into my Forester, my eyes flew to the empty back seat. "Where's Justin?"

"I tried to wave at you through the windshield," Julia answered. "He saw Jenny across the street, standing there watching us like an angry wet rabbit."

"Did he talk to her?"

"He went after her and she took off that way. East." Julia gestured at the back window. "He heard every word you said about that girl."

"How did he react?" I asked.

153

"He said you were wrong and he was going to prove it. He could hardly walk, Rachel."

"No, no." I rubbed my fingers over my eyes, angry with myself for not keeping an eye on him.

"Jenny would never hurt him," Olivia said with authority. "It's not going to happen. She—"

"Loves him?" I finished, turning to glare at her. "And he loves her, doesn't he?

Her eyes wide as saucers, Olivia said, "How did you know?"

"First, the way he talks about her. Second, no restaurant owner messes with proven menu success unless love is involved. And third, he kept to her menu even after his restaurant started losing customers. He told me he might reconsider, but I don't think so."

"Rachel writes mysteries," Julia said proudly.

The rain picked up, cascading down the windows and pounding on the Forester's hood.

"Those two are out in this rain," Julia said.

I fixed my eyes on Olivia and spoke slowly and deliberately, emphasizing each word. "Where would Jenny be leading Justin?"

Looking shell-shocked, she opened her mouth to speak, but nothing came out.

"This is no time to think of yourself. Not if you care about him."

"Her house is back that way," Olivia said.

"Right." I started the engine and sped from the curb.

Julia shouted over the thunder and rain that I was heading the wrong way.

"I'm going to the police station."

"That's right! The chief will know what to do!"

154

Bubbling with excitement, she gave her legs a slap. Women with dreadlocks in bright yellow houses? No. Loud Celtic music? No. A dangerous chase involving Chief Gilroy? Oh, yeah.

Two minutes later I screeched to a halt outside the police station and dashed inside, leaving the car running. Officer Underhill was at the front desk, half asleep with his chin in his hand.

"Good, you're here!" I shouted at him.

"Yeah? Not that I want to be," he said, rousing himself. "The chief told me to stay put."

"Where is he?"

"Out solving crime."

I planted my hands on the desk. "Where?"

"I don't keep tabs on him."

"Officer Underhill, you're overworked and tired, I get that, but this is an emergency. I need to know where Gilroy is."

Finally grasping that I was more than a little serious, Underhill stood, pushed the side button on his shoulder microphone, and called for Gilroy. Two seconds later I heard Gilroy's voice. He was at the Spruce Tavern, he said, bringing Tyler Hannaford in for questioning.

I leaned across the desk, grabbed hold of Underhill's shoulder, and yelled into his microphone. "Find Jenny Hannaford. She killed Maureen."

"Rachel?"

"Jenny killed Maureen," I repeated. "Tyler and Olivia set Maureen up to get back at her for harassing them, but I don't think they knew Jenny was going to kill her."

"Olivia Seitz was my next stop. Where are you?"

"At the station, Chief," Underhill said, prying my hand

from his shoulder and giving me a look that said, *Don't ever do that again.*

"What are you . . . ?" I heard Gilroy heave a sigh. "Stay there."

"You don't understand," I yelled at the top of my voice.

Underhill angled his shoulder my way. "Don't shout."

"Jenny is crazy," I told Gilroy. "She saw Olivia talking to Tyler and broke Olivia's windows, she saw me talking to Tyler in the Spruce Tavern and went ballistic, and just a few minutes ago, she saw me talking to Justin in my car. She loves him and she's going to kill him."

There was a pause on the other end of the microphone.

"Makes sense to me, Chief," Underhill said.

"Where did you see them last?" Gilroy said.

"Outside the Porter Grill, walking east. And Chief Gilroy, Justin is going through chemo. He's very weak."

There was another long pause before Gilroy spoke. "Stay at the station, Rachel. I mean it. I can't help Justin and worry about you at the same time. Got it?"

"Got it," I said. And I meant it. Jenny Hannaford was crazy. The sort of woman who could hold a grudge for decades and explode at the slightest provocation. I was happy to let Gilroy handle her, and he could find her and Justin faster in his police department SUV than I could in my Subaru.

"You're here too, Mrs. Foster?" Underhill said.

I wheeled back to the door.

"Olivia decided to take a walk in the rain," Julia said, shoving a hand into her damp gray hair and giving it a shake. "Or is it 'make a run for it'? I'm glad she didn't decide to take off in your car—with me in it." She dropped my car keys into my outstretched hand.

"Never mind, we'll get her," Underhill said. "How about some coffee?"

"I wouldn't say no," Julia said.

I told Underhill no, that I was wound up enough without the caffeine. I eyed the station clock.

"To think Holly is at home in bed," Julia said.

"Dry and snug."

"I wouldn't change places with her, would you?" Julia nudged me for what must have been the tenth time in a week. "I heard the chief say he couldn't help Justin and *worry* about you at the same time."

Underhill threw me a sideways glance as he handed Julia a mug of coffee.

"I hope Justin is okay," I said, committed to ignoring her Gilroy jabs. "He loves Jenny and trusts her, in spite of everything."

"If anyone can find him, the chief can," Julia said.

Underhill retired to his spot behind the front desk. "You think a lot of him, don't you?" he asked Julia.

"You weren't here before he became chief," Julia said. "We couldn't keep a chief or an officer for more than a year. No one wanted to stay. Everyone wanted to go to Fort Collins or Loveland or Denver. Chief Gilroy actually likes it here. He cares about the town and the people."

I tilted my head Julia's way. "She's his biggest fan."

"I'm a sensible woman," she said, poking my side with her elbow.

Half an hour passed before Gilroy strode through the station door, Jenny Hannaford in tow. Both were soaking wet, and Jenny was in handcuffs, snarling like a cornered cat.

"Tyler Hannaford is outside," Gilroy said to Underhill,

tossing him the keys. Without even a tip of the chin to me and Julia, he disappeared down the station hall. Officer Underhill scrambled around the desk and made for the door.

A minute later Underhill returned with Tyler, who was visibly agitated but not quite as wet or snarling as Jenny.

"Do you know how long I've been sitting in that car?" he complained. "You could have asked me to come down to the station. And why is my wife in handcuffs?

Because she's acting like a madwoman, I thought.

"You're here?" Tyler said, looking my way.

"Is Justin all right?" I asked.

"You mean my so-called friend?" Tyler said, as Underhill pulled him toward the hall. "He ratted on Jenny the second Gilroy appeared, but yeah, he's just fine."

Underhill too disappeared, leaving me and Julia in the suddenly silent lobby. For the first time that night, I felt the cold and damp, especially across my shoulders where the rain had seeped through my jacket. We waited several minutes, but neither Gilroy nor Underhill returned. Except for the occasional faint and childish wail from Jenny, we might have been the only ones in the station.

"You did it again," Julia whispered. "You solved the murder."

I smiled back at her. "Let's go."

I left the station and hurried for my car, my shoulders hunched against the rain.

CHAPTER 19

Saturday morning broke clear and crisp, a perfect autumn day. I rose early, and after a long and lazy breakfast of eggs, coffee, and toast, I headed to the garden center, east of downtown. I slowed to a crawl as I neared the Porter Grill, and I caught sight of Justin Miller drinking coffee outside, sitting on one of the restaurant's chairs, his feet resting on a planter.

I braked, rolled down my window, and waved, and he raised his coffee mug and shouted a good morning. He was going to be all right. Sure, he loved Jenny, or had been falling back in love with her, but last night any illusions he'd had about her had been shattered—before it was too late. I didn't know what the future held for him, but it didn't hold Jenny Hannaford, and that was a blessing.

After making my purchase at the garden center, I stopped by Holly's Sweets and bought four almond scones. Holly wiggled her finger at me, signaling me to come around the counter. I set my box on the microwave and peered into the back of the bakery, where Caleb and Matt Ward were cleaning the floors—and jousting good-naturedly at each other with the mops.

"I heard about last night," Holly said.

"Already?"

"I told you, this is Juniper Grove's Grand Central Station. I heard the moment the doors opened. Did Gilroy thank you profusely?"

"Nah, he was too busy."

"He had two perps to handle and a third one on the loose."

"Perps?" I said with a laugh.

"Crime talk. If we're going to keep doing this, we need to get our terminology straight."

I nodded at Caleb and Matt. "Lucky you, to have such good help."

"They're going to end up being friends at school, not just here. Where are you off to?"

"I have some errands to run. Have a good day off tomorrow."

After leaving the bakery, I drove west to Gina Peeler's house, hoping to find her on her porch. I did. In her usual spot with a mug of tea in her hands.

She smiled, motioned for me to come through her gate, and spread her arms out, presenting her restored yellow house. The sheets of plywood were gone, every window had been replaced, and the window trim had been painted in a Gina-like bright orange.

"What do you think?" she said. Her eyes were alight.

"They did it so fast."

"They said Chief Gilroy was on them to get it done quickly, so they brought a large crew yesterday. I didn't know they were going to paint the trim too. They asked me what color I wanted, I said bright orange, they bought it in Loveland, and there you go." Her gaze dropped to the pink box in my hand.

"These are for you," I said. "Almond scones."

"You didn't have to do that! Come on up here, right now. Let's have some tea and scones."

"This is yours too," I said, mounting the porch steps.

She took the bag from my hand, gave the garden center logo a puzzled look, and opened it. "Oh my."

"It's the only bamboo wind chime they had."

"It's perfect."

"I'll hang it up before I go."

"Thank you, Rachel. This is so wonderful, I hardly know what to say. Olivia thought she was hurting me, but she ended up making my life better. Not that she wanted to."

"Olivia's not going to be bothering you anymore," I said. I spent the next few minutes catching Gina up on the previous night's excitement. At one point she stopped me to let me know my recitation of events was "better than television."

"I don't know what's going to happen to Olivia and Tyler," I said, "but Jenny is going away for a very long time."

"Maybe the rest of her life," Gina said.

"I think so."

Gina leaned back and exhaled deeply, as if she were expelling thoughts of Jenny and her friends along with her breath.

"Let's not talk about them anymore," I said.

"It's a beautiful fall day."

"Halloween's back on for tonight, I heard."

Gina dipped into the bakery box and grabbed a scone. "Want one?" she asked.

I laid my hand on my stomach. "I'm stuffed. I had a

cream puff after breakfast."

"Fabulous!"

We sat quietly, listening to the rustle of the leaves in the light breeze, enjoying the scent of wood smoke from a neighbor's fireplace or woodstove. For the first time since the night of the scavenger hunt, I felt completely at ease. No clenched jaw, no nagging, anxious thoughts. My muscles unwound and I slouched happily in my seat. Minutes later I was about to close my eyes when a police SUV slid along the curb and stopped outside Gina's house.

"That's Chief Gilroy," Gina said, waving him through the gate.

I protested his arrival with a groan and sat straight.

Gilroy trudged up to the porch, a garden center bag in his hand. "Glad I caught you, Mrs. Peeler," he said.

"I'm not likely to be anyplace else, Chief."

"Rachel," Gilroy said, giving me a quick tip of his chin.

"Thank you so much for helping me," Gina said. "Look what they did!" Again she spread her arms, introducing him to her new-and-improved house. "And they gave me bright orange trim—some of my neighbors will have conniptions!"

Gilroy laughed. I couldn't remember the last time I'd seen him laugh.

"Have you got what I think you've got?" Gina said, pointing a long, thin finger at his garden center bag. "Rachel brought me something in the same bag."

"Oh?" He walked up the porch steps and held out the bag. "Just a housewarming gift. I guess you could call it that."

She stuck out her hands and eagerly wiggled her fingers. "This is so exciting!"

Gilroy sat in the plastic chair next to mine and watched,

with unconcealed pleasure, as Gina opened her bag and pulled out another wind chime.

"It is!" she cried. "Oh, I've got two wind chimes now, just like before."

"I'm sorry it's not bamboo," he said. "They didn't have any."

"That's because Rachel bought the last of them," she said. She gestured at the other bag.

"Did she?" Gilroy looked my way.

"They only had one bamboo one left," I said. *Brilliant, Rachel.*

A faint smile played on his lips. I wanted him to turn away, to stop looking at me with those eyes.

"You left before I could thank you last night," he said.

"You were busy."

"If this keeps up, I might have to hire you as my third officer."

"Rachel would make an incredible police office," Gina said, reaching into the bakery box for a second scone. "Chief, would you like a scone?"

"No, thank you."

"You're skin and bones, you need to eat."

"I had breakfast, thank you."

Skin and bones. And there I was, sitting in a plastic chair too small for my literally puffy frame.

"How about tea?" Gina asked.

"That would be nice," Gilroy said. He helped her from her chair, but when he tried to walk her inside, she shooed him away with a sweep of her hand and instructed him to sit.

"No use arguing with Gina," I said as he retook his seat. "She's sweet, but she's bossy."

"She knows her own mind, that's for sure."

"She's deliriously happy about her new windows and trim. How did you get the installers to move so fast?"

He shrugged. "I just asked."

I couldn't help but laugh. "Police chiefs don't ask, they make requests."

"What's the difference?"

"Requests are carried out."

"I'll have to remember that."

With our conversation going relatively well, meaning I wasn't tripping over my tongue and Gilroy wasn't speaking in one-syllable grunts, I decided to ask about last night. "Where did you find Justin and Jenny?"

"Outside the post office."

"Why were they there?"

"They were arguing on the sidewalk and happened to stop there. Jenny wanted to know why Justin was talking to you in your car. He told her, she admitted to killing Maureen Nicholson, and he didn't react as she'd hoped."

"Meaning he wasn't happy?"

"As soon as I caught up with them, he told me what she'd said. He couldn't get away fast enough."

"Poor Justin. I think he was falling in love with her. Or maybe he always was a little in love with her."

"Jenny said she killed Maureen because she loves Justin and couldn't stand to see what was happening to his business and his health."

"I think his cancer diagnosis was what set her off. She had to stop Maureen from harassing him because this time his health and life were at stake."

"You're probably right."

"Why were you bringing in Olivia and Tyler?"

"When they were in high school they pulled a nasty

164

prank on Maureen."

"With her prom dress."

He arched an eyebrow. "So you know about that too? It seemed to me they were acting together again. Covering for each other. There were too many coincidences. But what really did it was that blue flash drive."

"Did you find fingerprints or DNA?"

"No."

"But it was empty, wasn't it? I was sure it was."

"To the average eye, yes. But I took it to a computer forensics investigator, and he was able to retrieve deleted files."

I gaped. "You've got to be kidding me."

Gilroy nodded and chuckled. "It was loaded with inventory records from Blooms."

I shook my head, astonished that something so mundane had helped solve the case. "I never thought one of them would be foolish enough to use an old flash drive."

"Well, it lends credence to Olivia's argument that she didn't know Jenny was going to murder Maureen. If she'd known, she would have given Jenny a fresh drive."

"She can use it in court. 'Your honor, I'm not that stupid.'"

Gilroy chuckled again.

"So Olivia admitted to giving Jenny the flash drive?" I asked.

"She's admitted to everything, except knowing that Jenny was going to kill Maureen."

"Why did they even use an actual drive? Why didn't they just promise Maureen information and then not give it to her?"

"Jenny pushed for using the drive—I suspect because

165

she could strike while Maureen's attention was on it." He shrugged. "But in the end, I think it was just a part of their game."

"That's what Julia said. They went to the lengths they did because it was fun and annoyed Maureen."

"Julia's instincts can be scary," he said with a grin.

"I didn't think of it. Investigating the drive, I mean."

"I didn't think to look at Jenny's real motivation, or Justin's health."

A short pause in the conversation was broken by the sound of Gina clanging mugs together as she opened the screen door. Gilroy leaped up and went for the door, taking the mugs from her hands, and then went inside for Gina's old Brown Betty teapot.

When he came back out, he insisted on pouring the tea, to Gina's delight. And he told her as she settled into her chair that he would hang the wind chimes for her before he left. Gina returned to her half-eaten scone and seemed to revel in Gilroy's care and attention.

"Thank you, Chief. Rachel offered to hang hers, but I don't want her on a ladder."

"No, that's not a good idea."

"I stand on ladders all the time," I retorted.

"Do you like cinnamon, Chief Gilroy?" Gina asked. "The tea's chock-full of it."

"I could give it a go."

"You're coffee drinkers, the both of you. I can tell coffee drinkers."

"Guilty as charged," Gilroy said.

"Same here," I said.

Gilroy turned to me, and in a tone both offhanded and practiced, asked, "Want to go out for coffee sometime?"

"I think that's a fabulous idea," Gina said.

Had I been wrong about Gilroy? Had Officer Underhill sensed something in his dealings with me that I hadn't—or had refused to sense?

"Or not," Gilroy said.

"Sure," I said quickly. "I'd love to."

"Great. I'll give you a call." He held his mug to his nose and sniffed. "Mrs. Peeler, this smells dangerous."

"It is," I said. "It'll clear your sinuses."

Things were changing, I could feel it. Something was dragging me out of my private little world and pushing me into another, better world. I was ready.

FROM THE AUTHOR

We all need a place to escape to from time to time. A place where neighbors drink cups of coffee around a kitchen table (and some indulge in cream puffs), where friends feel safe sharing their hearts' deepest yearnings, where neighbors stop to chat with neighbors outside flower shops. True, the occasional murder mars the Juniper Grove landscape, but what would a mystery series be without dead bodies? Juniper Grove is still that place of escape, and I hope you'll join me there for all the books in the series. I look forward to sharing more of Rachel Stowe and her friends with you.

If you enjoyed *Death of a Scavenger*, please consider leaving a review on Amazon. Nothing fancy, just a couple sentences. Your help is appreciated more than I can say. Reviews make a huge difference in helping readers find the Juniper Grove Mystery Series and in allowing me to continue to write the series. Thank you!

KARIN'S MAILING LIST

For giveaways, exclusive content, and the latest news on the Juniper Grove Mystery Series and future Karin Kaufman books, sign up to the mail and newsletter list at KarinKaufman.com.

OTHER BOOKS IN THE JUNIPER GROVE MYSTERY SERIES

Death of a Dead Man
Death of a Scavenger
At Death's Door
Death of a Santa
Scared to Death
Cheating Death

MORE BOOKS BY KARIN KAUFMAN

ANNA DENNING MYSTERY SERIES

The Witch Tree
Sparrow House
The Sacrifice
The Club
Bitter Roots
Anna Denning Mystery Series Box Set: Books 1-3

CHILDREN'S BOOKS (FOR CHILDREN AND ADULTS)

The Adventures of Geraldine Woolkins

Made in the USA
San Bernardino, CA
25 November 2018